A SUMMER TOGETHER

LEGACY SERIES
BOOK 13

PAULA KAY

CONTENTS

ONE

Blu looked out the window as she waited for Jemma to join her for the coffee that she'd just poured for them. She could see Rafael and the kids in the distance below, building what looked to be a huge sand castle. She took a sip of her coffee and smiled when the light breeze from the open window hit her face just right. It felt good to be back there—at their beach house in La Jolla.

"Penny for your thoughts." Jemma grinned from across the small table as she slid into her chair and reached for her coffee. "This smells wonderful, thanks."

"Did you sleep well? Did you miss your old bedroom?"

The last time they'd been at the beach house together, Jemma and Rafael hadn't had the twins yet, so they'd slept in Jemma's old bedroom. Now, with the addition of four children to their family, Blu had set them up in an entirely different wing of the house where they'd have plenty of bathrooms and privacy. It was a part of the big house that Jemma had barely even been in as a child, so her reaction had been quite funny.

Jemma laughed in response to the question. "Well, I

suppose I'd be lying if I said I didn't miss my old bed just a bit. It felt weird not to be sleeping down the hall from Kylie." She looked at the time on her phone. "Speaking of Kylie, where is she, by the way?"

"Oh, she spent the night with one of her friends down here —another model. They went to a party last night and Kylie texted me around midnight to see if she could stay." Blu laughed when she saw the look on Jemma's face, knowing instantly her thoughts. "What? Don't act like you never stayed out until midnight when you were seventeen."

"Mom." Jemma set her coffee cup down. "First of all, she's sixteen. She's not seventeen yet for months. And second of all, yeah, I did stay out until midnight—and later—but when I did, I was disobeying my curfew. Does Kylie not have one or what?"

Blu raised an eyebrow and took another sip of coffee. Kylie was not Jemma. Kylie had never given her and Chase a fraction of the worry that Jemma had caused as a teen.

Jemma laughed when Blu didn't respond to her question. "Okay, point taken. I know Kylie is not the wild child that I was back then, but just be careful. You know, it's easy for things to get out of hand at that age and all these new friends, parties, this whole crazy world of modeling that she's suddenly been thrust into—I know you know all about that, so I'm sorry if I'm over-stepping. I don't mean to. I just—"

Blu reached across the table for Jemma's hand. "I know, honey. And your concerns are valid. You don't need to apologize for looking out for your sister."

"Okay, and I know Kylie's such a great kid, she always has been. I just hope we get to spend lots of time together while we're all here."

"I'm sure you will, honey. She knows that Gabby and

everyone is coming this afternoon, so she's under the strictest of orders to be back before three." Blu winked at Jemma.

"Okay, okay." Jemma's phone flashed with a text. "It's Lia. She says she tried to call you. Apparently they're trying to get Antonio in for a doctor's appointment before they leave. She says they switched their flight to tomorrow afternoon—so did Gigi and Douglas. Bella and Thomas are coming this afternoon as planned and Gabby is coming with them."

"Oh yeah? I hope everything's okay." Blu wasn't sure why, but she felt the slightest of knots in her stomach. She couldn't bear the thought of anything happening to one of them. Lia and Antonio were family to her, as much so as if they were related by blood.

"Everything will be fine, Mom."

Blu smiled at Jemma. "I'm sure you're right. I'll give Lia a call this morning—just to be sure."

"Mom?"

"Yes?"

"Don't worry, okay? This is supposed to be a relaxing time for you. Let's not make problems where there are none."

Blu laughed. "Who's making problems? Not this girl. And speaking of relaxing, what are your plans for today?"

Jemma stared out the window at her family and laughed. "Well, assuming that huge pile of sand I see down there by the kids is their father, Rafael said something about taking the kids to the park. Would you like to join us?"

"Thanks for the invite. I have a few things yet to do before everyone arrives. And I'm meeting Chase for lunch at one. He's out early this morning, playing golf with an old buddy of his." Blu laughed when she saw the expression on Jemma's face. "What?"

"It's just nice to see you two relaxing here. I mean, I never thought I'd see the day when Chase was off just playing golf. It's nice. You two deserve it for all the hard work you've put in over the years."

"Yes, well, I must say that life has gotten just a bit less stressful since we've slowed down to enjoy it. Which reminds me, did you check out the painting space I created for you upstairs?" Blu grinned thinking about the easels and paints she'd purchased the day before. She knew that it had been ages since Jemma had picked up her paintbrush, and Blu was hoping that maybe she'd be able to find the time while she was there this summer.

Jemma got up from the table to come around and give her a big hug. "I did, thank you. It's beautiful, and I'm definitely going to paint something while we're here. I can't wait, in fact."

"Good, honey. I miss your art."

"Well, it's good to be back where it all began." Jemma grinned. "And on that note, I think maybe I should go rescue my husband from those wild children of ours. Keep me posted if you find anything out about Antonio, okay?"

"I will." Blu watched Jemma walk across the deck and down the steps toward the beach, the sun hitting her long blond hair just as it used to all those years ago.

Yes, it was good to be back at the beach.

TWO

Lia tried not to worry as she waited for the time to come for Antonio's doctor appointment. The clinic had managed to squeeze him in for the next morning. Antonio had—for the first time in a very long time—gotten a bit snippy with her when she'd insisted that she try to get him in to see a doctor if one were available. But she knew her husband and something seemed not quite right. He'd been sleeping more than normal, and Antonio hardly ever slept in or took naps.

"Excuse me. Grandma, can I have a cookie, please?"

Lia smiled when she heard her great-granddaughter's voice. Three-year-old Arianna was a happy distraction from her troubled thoughts. "Yes, sure you can, sweetie. Did you pack up all your toys like Mommy asked you to?"

Arianna nodded. "Yes, sure I did. And I also helped Daddy pack Sammy's animals and blankets. Daddy says I'm all ready to go on the plane. I can't wait to see Chloe and Daisy—oh, can we please bring cookies for them too? And the boys?"

Lia laughed as she placed a chocolate chip cookie on the table in front of where Arianna had climbed up on the chair.

"Yes, I think we can do that. Maybe one day this week we can do some baking at the beach house. Would you like that?"

Arianna nodded, her mouth full of cookie.

Isabella walked into the kitchen with a smiling Samuel in her arms. She leaned down to kiss Arianna on the head. "Good job with your packing, honey. And you know you need to have a sandwich or something too before we leave, okay?"

"Okay."

"Lia, would you mind holding Sam for a minute? I'm starving and in desperate need of a coffee." Isabella laughed.

Lia held her arms out. "Come here, lovely boy."

Samuel was one of the happiest babies Lia had ever seen. The child hardly ever cried and thought his big sister was hysterical most of the time.

Isabella came back over to the table with coffee and croissant in hand. "Yum. These are delicious."

"They're from Gigi's favorite new bakery down the road and yes, they are quite good."

"Where's Gabby—and Gigi, for that matter? Does Gabby know we're leaving soon?" Isabella laughed when she saw the look on Arianna's face. "Don't worry, sweetie. You still have a little time to play outside after you eat something besides that cookie." Isabella walked back over to the counter and started making a peanut butter sandwich.

"Gigi took Gabby to the mall to pick something up. I think Antonio is in the den with Douglas—probably complaining about me," said Lia.

"What? No, you're kidding, right?" Isabella placed the sandwich in front of Arianna at the table. "Eat this, then you can go outside and play."

Arianna looked up at Lia as she took the sandwich in her

hand. "Why is Grandpa complaining about you, Grandma? And also, what does complaining mean?"

Lia and Isabella looked at one another and laughed.

"I have an idea, big girl. Why don't I set you up outside at the table with your sandwich?" Isabella winked at Lia.

"And can I have some lemonade too?" Arianna said.

"Of course. I've got it." Lia walked over to the fridge with an inquisitive Samuel on her hip watching her every move.

"Do you want me to take him now?" Isabella said as she came in from outside.

"No, it's okay. I like holding the little guy."

Samuel giggled as if he knew he was being talked about and the two women sat back down at the table.

"So, is everything okay? You don't really think something's wrong, do you? I mean, I overheard him telling you that he felt just fine—and well, I mean, he's as fit as they come, so I'd be shocked is all."

"I know. You're right. I'm sure he's fine. I just want him to see the doctor—if for no other reason than to ease my mind."

"Okay. I figured. And he's not really upset with you then."

"Well, he's not particularly happy about having to go to the doctor, but he'll get over it." Lia laughed. "We do get quite stubborn in our old age, I suppose."

Isabella reached out to pat her hand across the table. "I don't know what you're talking about. I don't know anyone around here who fits the description of old." She winked, then stood up from the table. "Sorry, but I think I'd better keep moving. I still need to pack, myself. I left Thomas upstairs on a phone call, so I'm not sure how much help he's being. I can take Sam with me, but would you mind keeping an eye on Arianna?"

"Not in the least, and leave Sammy with me too." She looked the little boy in the eyes. "We'll go outside to visit with your big sister. Would you like that?"

Isabella leaned over and kissed Lia on the cheek. "Thank you. And I'm sure everything's going to be just fine. You two will be with us at the beach in no time, your mind at ease and ready to party."

Lia laughed. "It's been so wonderful being here with everyone again, and it's going to be equally as good to get some much-needed beach time. You go ahead."

"I will, thank you. Send Arianna up when she's finished eating if you like."

"I'm sure we'll be fine. Take your time, honey."

THREE

Isabella smiled as she watched Gabriela and Arianna head into the shop at the airport hand in hand.

"Gabby is so good with her, isn't she?" she said to Thomas, who was sitting next to her with Samuel asleep in his arms. "Honey, are your arms getting tired? Do you want me to take him from you?"

"No, that's okay. And yes, Gabby is a dream." Thomas leaned over to kiss her lightly on the cheek.

"Lia says that she'd like to get some babysitting jobs over the summer," said Isabella.

Thomas grinned. "And you told her?"

"Of course I told her that with all the kids we have between us, there'd be no need for outside jobs. I'm pretty sure we can keep her busy enough. And Kylie too, although it sounds like she's pretty busy with work and her social calendar these days—well, that's what Jemma tells me.

"Even in San Diego?"

"Yeah, I guess so. Jemma says she has a few friends from modeling there."

"That's nice. Isn't it?" Thomas raised his eyebrow.

"What?"

"Well, you have a funny look on your face."

"Oh, I just hope that Gabby's going to feel included. She's more shy than Kylie around new people, I think."

"Honey, I'm sure they'll be fine. You know as well as I do that Kylie and Gabby are practically attached at the hip."

"Yeah, you're right. Anyway, here they come." She leaned over to brush his lips with a quick kiss just as Gabriela and Arianna walked up.

"Mommy, why are you and Daddy always kissing?" Arianna giggled as she walked over to the chair and dumped the contents of the bag she carried. "I picked out lots of fun things to do on the plane—a book, some cards, a little treasure—oh, and Gabriela let me get some gum. Is that okay?"

"Well, it is good for airplane rides." Gabriela shrugged and laughed. "Sorry if she went a little crazy there."

Isabella laughed. "Yes, that's fine. And honey, you know our plane ride is very short—not like the long one we took from Italy."

"Yes, I know. But that's okay. When we get to the beach, I'm going to share all my stuff with Chloe and Daisy—and Mommy, they love chewing gum also."

"Okay, that's good, honey. Now, why don't you move your things over so Gabby can sit down here too?"

Arianna obeyed and Gabriela sat down next to Isabella.

"Are you excited to go to the beach, Gabby?"

Gabriela nodded and brought her phone up to look at it. "I am. I've been trying to get a hold of Kylie all day though. She's not answering my texts or my phone calls, so I guess she must have a modeling job or something."

"Probably so. Kylie's mom mentioned to me that she has a pretty busy week scheduled. But you know how much the kids love it when you play with them, so hopefully when Kylie's busy you'll come play with us at the beach."

"Will you, Gabby?" Arianna asked.

"Of course." Gabriela smiled at Arianna. "Do you want me to read your new book to you?"

"Oh yes, that would be great!" said Arianna.

Isabella looked from Gabriella to Thomas. "If you two don't mind, I think I'm going to take a little walk and try to give Jemma a call." She looked at her phone. "We still have at least an hour before boarding."

"Go ahead, honey," said Thomas.

Isabella pulled up Jemma's number as she walked away toward a quieter section of the boarding area. Jemma answered on the third ring after a second of silence and what sounded like a big gulp of air.

"Bella? You're saving me." She laughed

"Well, that sounds either horrifying or fun, but because you're laughing, I'm thinking that my best friend has not just been kidnapped and held for ransom."

"Nothing quite that exciting—just my kids chasing me around the playground, but I tagged out with Rafael. Where are you guys? Your flight leaves soon, yes?"

"Yep, in about an hour or so. We're due there at five."

"Excellent. I think Chase is planning to barbecue tonight, although maybe with the change of plans, we'll do that tomorrow instead. Bella, how's Lia? Are they really doing okay? I mean, I know it's probably nothing, but I feel like she must be worried or something."

"Yeah—I mean I think everything's okay. I think they just

don't want to leave town without having a chat with the doctor, you know—just to be sure. Well, that's how Lia made it sound to me anyway."

"Okay. I can't wait until you're here! And the girls are driving me nuts. They keep asking when Arianna is arriving. You'd think that it wasn't just a few nights ago that they were all together having a slumber party."

Isabella smiled. She loved how close the girls were. Sometimes Arianna referred to them as her cousins, which always tugged at Isabella's heart just a bit. But she couldn't be too bothered by the fact that Arianna didn't have blood-related cousins. How could she be when their extended family—the one created out of love and circumstance—gave them everything they could ever need in terms of love and support?

"Well, Arianna's the same. She's been counting down the hours and she's just bought a whole bunch of goodies to share with the girls. Don't worry about dinner if Chase wants to wait on that until tomorrow. We can order pizza or whatever. I'm just anxious to dig my feet in the sand next to my best friend— maybe work on my nonexistent tan just a bit."

"I'm looking forward to that too. Hey, I gotta run. I'm pretty sure that one of the girls is now stuck up in a tree."

"Oh, goodness!" Isabella laughed. "You go. I'll see you in a few hours."

"Bye, Bella. See you soon."

FOUR

Jemma laughed, slightly winded as Rafael chased her across the grass.

"I give up! I give up!"

"Why do you give up so easily, my love?"

He whispered the words in her ear as his arms came around her and he playfully tackled her to the ground.

She brought her lips up to meet his, thankful for the chance to catch her breath, while at the same time just as willing to lose it again if it meant getting lost in the kisses of her husband—something she never seemed to tire of.

"Ewww. You guys are always kissing!"

Jemma grinned as she saw Nicolas out of the corner of her eye. And just as quickly Mateo hit his brother lightly on the arm.

"You're it, Nick! Go get Chloe. She's over on the big slide."

The boys ran off. Jemma asked, "Do you think we should go over by them?"

Rafael looked back to where the kids were all now congregated at the top of the slide. "Nah, let's enjoy a moment while they seem to have occupied themselves." He kissed her again and then looked at her in a funny way.

"What? Why are you looking at me so crazy?" She grinned, enjoying their flirtation.

"Not crazy, darling, unless you mean crazy for you." He wiggled his eyebrows in that goofy way that Jemma loved. "Jem, you look kinda tired."

"I am tired, now that you mention it." She moved to sit up, Rafael taking her hand to sit beside her. "Well, let's let the kids play for a while longer. Soon Bella and everyone will be here and we can go back to the house and order pizza or something." She reached into her jeans pocket when her phone buzzed with an incoming text.

"What is it?" Rafael smoothed her hair back from her face as she thought about her response.

"Kylie. She's being a bit of a punk." She laughed lightly, but it didn't help her to feel less annoyed at her sister.

"Why, what's she done?"

"Well, you've probably noticed that she hasn't been around at all since we got here. Mom told me earlier that she'd promised to be here before Gabby arrives."

"Okay, and...?"

"And she just texted asking me to let Mom know that she's spending the night at her friend's house again—that she'll be home early in the morning." Jemma frowned. "That's really not cool."

"Well, part of me is thinking that she's just being a teenager —you know?"

"Right. But Raf, you know Kylie, she's—"

"I know. She doesn't normally put anything before family, and it kinda seems like that's what she's doing."

"Exactly, and especially because she knows Gabby is coming. I dunno. I don't really want to fight with her."

Rafael kissed her quickly on the end of the nose. "You two never fight. Call her." He got to his feet and held out his hand for Jemma to take. "I'll go tell the kids they have about fifteen more minutes."

Jemma let Rafael help her to her feet. "Okay. Good idea. Thanks, honey."

She pulled up Kylie's number on her phone and walked a few feet to sit down on one of the park benches while it rang. When it went to voice mail, she sighed, hung up, and sat for a second before composing a text.

Feeling irritated at her sister was the last thing Jemma wanted, and it was abnormal. Kylie had always been the best little sister and Jemma knew that she didn't have a real reason to be concerned about her. It was this whole new world of modeling that had Jemma even thinking the thoughts about her sister changing in some way. But she should trust that Kylie was still the same sweet girl she'd always been.

She smiled as her phone rang, Kylie's name popping up on the screen.

"Hey, you. I miss you."

"Hi, Jem."

She seemed to pause for a moment to get her breath.

"Sorry, I was in the other room when you called and didn't make it to my phone on time. Did you get my text?"

"I did. Yes. How come you're not calling Mom yourself?"

"Oh, please, Jemma. Can't you just tell her? She won't mind. I've been at a shoot all day and I never get to hang out with Whitney. I promise I'll be home in the morning first thing."

15

"Who's Whitney?"

"She's just a girl that I know from a show we did together in Milan. She's so cool. Jem, you'd love her."

Jemma's heart tugged a little, hearing the excitement in Kylie's voice. Rafael was right. She was just being a teenager, excited about spending time with her new friends. Jemma shouldn't be so hard on her sister.

"Well, maybe you can bring Whitney around the house so we can meet her."

"Yeah, I will. That's a good idea."

"Kylie, you do remember that Gabby arrives today, yeah?"

The phone went silent for a few seconds.

"Darn. Well, I did know that, but I forgot. I need to text Gabby. She won't mind, will she, Jem?"

Jemma felt relieved to hear the concern in Kylie's voice. She knew that if she pushed it with her sister, she'd come home. She wouldn't want to hurt Gabby's feelings.

"No, don't worry about it. But text her. I'll tell Mom and I'm sure Gabby will be fine hanging out with the kids tonight. But Kylie, you are planning to be around, aren't you? This is supposed to be a family vacation."

"Yeah, I know. I will be. Don't worry. Okay, I gotta run. Kiss the kids for me and tell them I'll see them in the morning."

Jemma smiled. "I will. Have fun. And Kylie—"

Kylie hung up before Jemma could finish her sentence.

"You be careful." Her voice was quiet as she said the words that only she could hear.

FIVE

Blu smiled at her husband as he crossed the kitchen with two cups of coffee in his hands.

"Here you go, honey."

She took it from him and savored her first sip. "Why does my coffee taste so much better when you make it?"

Chase reached for her hand across the small breakfast table. "Because I am an expert chef and for you, I add my special ingredient." He sat up slightly from his seat so that he could kiss her on the mouth. "My special ingredient of passion, *mi amor.*"

Blu laughed as he sat back down. "I love you, goofball— even more than I do this coffee right now." She winked.

They sat in easy silence for a few minutes, Blu enjoying the slight ocean breeze coming through the open windows where they sat. The little breakfast nook off the kitchen had always been one of her favorite spaces in the beach house and it felt good sitting here now with her husband.

"So why are we both up so early this morning anyway?" Chase asked, taking another sip of his coffee.

Blu grinned. "Well, we both know why you're up—Mister Start Every Morning with a Run."

And he was dressed for a run, so Blu knew she was right about that. Ever since Chase had left the restaurant, he'd become quite the morning person, something Blu still wasn't used to. Typically, back home in Italy, by the time she got out of bed, Chase would have a nice breakfast prepared after he'd already gotten his run in, so it was unusual for her to be up just after sunrise.

He grinned at her. "Wanna join me?"

It was a standing joke between them—Blu constantly talking about getting into a regular exercise routine, then balking when Chase invited her to join him for anything more strenuous than a stroll along the beach.

"No thanks, babe. Maybe tomorrow." She winked. "I had a hard time sleeping—finally decided to just get up and start the day, I guess."

"Is it Kylie? Are you upset with her for not coming home last night?"

"Well, I am a little miffed that she couldn't call me to speak to me about it. That's not like her and it makes me question—at least a little bit—these new friends that she has here. Honey, we might need to reel her in a little bit—"

"Blu."

"Yeah."

"Kylie is not Jemma." He reached for her hand across the table, giving it a squeeze. "Just because we're back here, don't let old memories cloud your judgment."

"Funny you should bring up Jemma. She's the one that got me even having any thoughts about Kylie's behavior in the first place. But Jemma does have a point that Kylie has changed a little bit—case in point, her not being here last night to greet Gabby and the others."

Chase nodded. "I agree. That is unlike her, to be sure. It's just nothing to cause the alarm bells to ring. What time is she supposed to be home, then?"

"She did finally text me, promising she'd be here no later than nine this morning, so I guess I'll feel better after that."

"I'm sure you will. And I'm sure she'll be on time, honey." Chase got up from the table to come around and kiss Blu on the neck just as she heard someone coming down the stairs in the other room.

"Morning." Gabby grinned at them from the doorway of the kitchen, like Blu, still in her pajamas. "I thought I heard voices down here. I thought it might be Kylie."

Chase looked at his watch. "Kylie should be here soon. Gabby, help yourself to coffee—do you drink coffee these days? I'll see you guys after my run."

"Have a good run." Blu got up from the table. "Gabby, honey, have a seat. Let me get you something. What do you like in the morning? Kylie just recently started drinking coffee, but before that she was all about hot chocolate."

"Yes, please. That sounds great."

Blu put some water on to boil and then sat down at the table across from the young girl. Gabby was practically a part of their family. She couldn't remember a time when Kylie and Gabby weren't inseparable, and she found herself hoping that this wasn't going to change anytime soon. She willed the thought away as she looked at her now staring out the window toward the ocean.

"Did you sleep okay last night or was the slumber party a mistake?"

The three little girls had begged and pleaded to sleep in the upstairs rec room together and then they all wanted Gabby to join them.

"Those girls. I didn't think they were ever going to go to sleep. What chatterboxes!"

Blu laughed. "Well, I know they are very excited to be reunited."

"Very." Gabby laughed too. "Blu, do you know what time my parents are coming today?"

"I think it won't be too late this afternoon. Are you doing okay, honey? You know, you can ask me for anything you need."

"I know. Thank you. I'm just anxious for Kylie to get home. We've been playing phone tag lately—well, mostly it's me calling her, I guess." She laughed lightly. "So I just can't wait to catch up with her. We've been looking forward to being at the beach together for weeks now."

Blu got up to make the hot chocolate, returning to set the steaming cup on the table in front of Gabby.

"And I know Kylie has been looking forward to having you here as well."

"Yes, she has!"

Blu and Gabby both looked up at the sound of Kylie's voice as she made her way across the room with a big grin on her face.

"Kylie!" Gabby got up from the table to give her a hug and Blu quietly made her way over to the counter. "Wow, you're up and out early this morning."

"With good reason. Gabby, I'm really sorry I wasn't here last night. And I am glad you're here—so glad!"

Blu smiled from where she watched them from across the kitchen, preparing a second cup of hot chocolate for her daughter. Kylie was a good kid. Blu needed to not forget that and not borrow trouble where there was none.

She walked back to the table where the two now sat with their heads together looking at something on Kylie's phone.

"Here's some hot chocolate, honey."

Kylie looked like she was about to protest before glancing at Gabby's cup. "Yum! Thanks, Mom. And I'm really sorry I didn't call you yesterday. Do you forgive me?"

Blu leaned down to kiss her daughter's forehead. "Yes, I forgive you." She reached for her phone on the table. "I'll leave you two to catch up while I go outside to give Gigi a call."

"Thanks, Mom. Love you!" Kylie called after her, already in hysterics about something Gabby had said.

Blu shook her head and smiled as she made her way to the outside fireplace, which was already going with a nice fire thanks to her considerate husband.

SIX

Gigi smiled when she saw that it was Blu on the phone. Leave it to one or another of the women in her life to know when she was feeling anxious. After Lia and Antonio had left for his doctor appointment, Douglas had retreated to his office to take care of a few things and Gigi didn't want to bother him, so she'd settled for being alone with her thoughts.

"Hi." Gigi answered.

"Good morning. I really hope I'm not calling too early, but I thought it might be a good time to catch you."

"It's a perfect time, actually. Antonio's appointment is at eight thirty so we've all been up for awhile before they left. How are things there? Bella texted us last night that they got in okay."

"Well, it's pretty quiet around here right now. Definitely letting the girls sleep for as long as they will."

"I can't wait to get there. It's going to be a great time for all of us."

"Well, I won't keep you. I just wanted to check in and let you know that we're all anxious for you to get here."

"Thanks, honey. Yes, I know we'll all feel a lot better here after we know that everything is fine with Antonio. Lia hasn't been talking about it much, but I get the feeling that she's feeling more concerned than she's letting on."

"Well, I suppose she knows Antonio—the way he is day-to-day—probably more than he even recognizes in himself. I get that. If Chase were suddenly super tired or something else seemed odd for him, I'd be insistent about a doctor visit too."

"Yeah, same here, and Douglas knows that all too well."

Gigi smiled. She was the one that dutifully made their regular medical and dental appointments, and she was pretty confident that left to his own devices, Douglas couldn't care less—well, except for the fact that he wanted her to be healthy and around for a long time.

"Do you have big plans for the day there?"

"No real plans—just letting the kids play together, probably at the beach this afternoon."

"I'll text you after we land. Douglas has a car coming for us and I'd think we'd be there well before dinner."

"Okay, sounds good. See you later, Gigi."

Gigi clicked off the phone and looked out across the garden. It was slightly chilly this time of day, but she loved the way it smelled outside in this space—all fresh and fragrant, the flowers and plants just waking up to greet the morning sun.

It was always so quiet after the kids had been there for a few days. Gigi loved it best when the house was filled with the sounds of their playing and laughing together. And soon it would be the same thing, just at the beach house.

She looked at the time on her phone. 8:35. Hopefully, Antonio would get right in for his appointment—typically a plus, getting in early in the day before doctors have a chance to fall behind in their schedules.

She thought about her conversation with Blu. What *would* she ever do if something happened to Douglas? She could barely stand the thought, but of course the inevitable for both of them was coming whether they wanted it or not. Were there things that they had yet to do together? Places to go? Things to see?

Gigi knew these were dangerous thoughts to have, that she and Douglas had made plenty of choices over the years as to where to spend their time and who to spend it with. She knew there'd been no mistakes. She loved her life in Italy and she loved the family that she'd chosen to surround herself with.

"Penny for your thoughts, my darling."

Douglas's quiet words made her jump.

"Good grief! Way to almost give me a heart attack!" She turned around to embrace him, her heart still pounding fast as she did so.

"I'm sorry, dear. I wasn't trying to sneak up on you. I promise." He kissed her on the lips then pointed to the table a few feet away. "I brought our coffees out."

"Wow. I guess I must have been pretty zoned out there. Thank you, honey."

They sat down at the table together, Gigi taking a sip of her coffee that was just the way she liked it.

Douglas reached across the table for her hand. "So what had you so deep in thought? Is everything alright?"

Gigi smiled at her husband. He was always so sensitive to her feelings, something that always rather amazed her.

"Everything's fine. I just got off the phone with Blu. We were talking about how well we know our husbands when it comes to their health and well-being." She winked at him.

"Oh, you think so, do you?" He grinned back at her.

"I do. But I think you probably feel the same about me. You know, how we do such a good job of caring for one another?"

He brought her hand to his lips. "Yes, dear, we do enjoying taking care of each other, don't we?"

Gigi nodded, lost in her thoughts once again.

"And now?"

"Now?"

"What are you thinking about now, my love? I can see it on your face." He laughed and settled back in his chair some.

"Oh, I don't know. I guess I've just been thinking about our life together—how wonderful it's been—how great you've always been to me."

"Well, those are fine thoughts to be having this morning."

"They are, yes. And also—"

"Yes, dear?"

"We should be sure that there aren't still things that we want to do together—places we might want to visit—you know, that sort of thing."

"Honey, I'm pretty sure that we still have plenty of time to do lots of those things together. Is there something in particular you want to do? Some place you want to go? You know, I'll take you anywhere your little heart desires."

He was teasing her, and she loved him for making the thoughts in her head so much lighter. Yes, they did have time. She didn't need to focus on anything other than loving this man who'd made her so incredibly happy over the years that they'd shared together.

Gigi looked at her phone as it buzzed with an incoming text. "It's Lia. She says they're in the exam room now—just waiting on the doctor. Honey, I told her if they felt like it after, we'd meet them at the park. I figured you'd be up for a little exercise."

"Did you now?" Douglas grinned as he stood up. "Okay, let's see how they make out with the doctor. I'm just going to go take care of a few things then. Let me know when you're ready."

Gigi stood up to kiss Douglas. "I will. And I guess I should go get dressed myself."

SEVEN

Lia felt Antonio's hand on her knee right before he leaned over to kiss her on the cheek.

"Don't look so worried, my love. I'm sure everything is fine."

She tried to smile as she nodded her head, but inside, the concern she had just wouldn't go away. Now that they were sitting in the waiting room, she would have thought she'd feel better, but instead it only seemed to be making her feel more anxious.

There were only two other people sitting there besides them —an elderly man with a young girl—a caregiver, Lia imagined.

She reached over to squeeze Antonio's hand. "Thanks for agreeing to see the doctor, honey. I know you didn't want to."

"I'm sorry I yelled at you—the other day. I know I can be stubborn, but you didn't deserve that—"

"Antonio. Stop. You don't need to apologize again."

The look in his eyes said everything. He was always so kind, so loving to her. Throughout their entire marriage it had been like that. He never for one second left her to wonder about his thoughts or feelings. She knew how lucky she was to be married to a man like that—how lucky they both were to have reconnected later in life to live out their one true love affair. She'd do anything to extend their years together, even if it meant Antonio's anger over a doctor visit insisted upon to ease her concerns.

They both looked up when the door to the waiting room opened and a woman stepped through looking down at a clipboard, before looking up to announce the lucky winner. It was the elderly man, so more waiting for them.

Lia glanced at Antonio, not missing the fact that he seemed to be holding his breath in. She looked at the time on her phone, for the first time noticing a text from Gabriela.

Good luck today. Kiss Dad for me. I'm sure it's nothing. I love you both. XO

She smiled as she showed the note to Antonio and almost immediately saw the crease in his forehead.

"Honey, I don't want Gabby to worry. I feel like this is all getting blown a little out of proportion."

Lia shook her head. "No, Gabby's fine. Don't you think it feels that way because we happen to be around everyone right now? If we were back home, your doctor visits would be—well, they'd be private."

"Yes, except I doubt you'd be any less worried, and I really doubt that you'd keep that worry to yourself, my dear." He winked at her, which made her laugh lightly.

"Okay, point taken. I guess I probably would confide in Gigi, but only so that I wouldn't drive you crazy talking about it." She handed him her phone. "Anyway, why don't you text Gabby back? Tell her I'll call her after the appointment."

Antonio took the phone, sent the text, and just as he was

handing it back to Lia, the woman with the clipboard appeared again, nodding to them. "Antonio? You can follow me."

Lia looked at him with a question in her eyes.

He stood up and reached for her hand, pulling her up beside him. "Well, let's get this over with."

She nodded and together they followed the woman to a waiting room where she took his vitals and asked a few questions of him before leaving them to wait for the doctor.

Lia pulled her phone out from her purse again. "I'll text Gigi to let her know we're just waiting on the doctor now. She had mentioned maybe meeting us after over by that park where we've been walking together this last week—that is, if you feel up to it, honey."

Antonio nodded and then got off the table where he'd been sitting to kiss Lia squarely on the lips. "I love you."

She looked into his eyes. "I love you too—so much."

They both sat down again, Lia on a chair against the wall, Antonio back on the examining table.

Just as she was sending the text to Gigi, there was a knock on the door, followed by the entrance of a smiling young doctor. He crossed the room to introduce himself as Dr. Rogers, shaking first Antonio's hand and then Lia's before he sat down to look at Antonio's chart.

"Okay, it looks like your blood pressure is quite elevated. Have you had any issues with it in the past? Are you on any medications?"

Antonio looked at Lia and they both shook their heads.

The doctor looked back at the notes and then to Antonio again. "And what brings you here today?"

"Well, honestly I feel fine. I mean, I'm not sick or anything, but my wife thinks I've been more tired than usual."

Lia nodded her head. "Yes, I just noticed some changes with him lately and—well, we're traveling tomorrow—just down to San Diego—and we want to be sure everything is fine—more for peace of mind, I suppose."

"Okay, that seems reasonable." Dr. Rogers walked over to listen to Antonio's heart, then sat back down in his chair. "Have you been having any shortness of breath lately? Anything else unusual."

Lia didn't miss the look that flashed across Antonio's face. There were things he'd not been telling her. She knew it in that instant. She held her breath while she waited for him to reply.

Antonio glanced at Lia quickly before he answered the doctor. "Yes, I suppose something has been a little off. I thought maybe it had to do with flying or something. It was only a few days ago that we flew here from Italy." He looked at Lia again. "So yes, I guess I have had some moments of feeling a little out of breath and..."

"Yes?" Dr. Rogers looked up from what he was writing on the chart.

"I have been having more indigestion than normal—you know, popping more of the chewables." He laughed lightly but this was definitely a surprise to Lia.

"I see." The doctor wrote something on his paper and then picked up the wall phone, speaking to someone about coming to their room. "I'm going to step out for a minute while you change into a gown. I'd like to get an EKG reading—so that we have a clearer picture of how your heart is doing."

Lia's heart beat faster as she watched Antonio take the paper gown that the doctor was handing him. "Doctor?"

He turned to look at her with his hand still on the door handle.

"What exactly are you looking for? On the EKG?"

"Well, that alone won't tell us for sure, but it will give a good indication if your husband"—his gaze shifted to Antonio—"if you've suffered any heart damage."

He looked back at Lia and she felt herself become light-headed as he spoke.

"The test will give us an indication if there's been a heart attack, but let's just take it one step at a time, okay?"

He smiled at her and she nodded.

And as soon as the door closed, Lia burst into tears.

EIGHT

Gigi watched Lia as she drove them to the park, her face tense, her fingers tight around the steering wheel. Gigi had gotten the text from her about thirty minutes ago.

Stopping by the house to drop Antonio off. Will you go for a walk with me?

Gigi had never even witnessed a cross word between Lia and Antonio, but in the short amount of time that it took for Antonio to exit the car and Gigi to enter it, the air around the couple had been thick with tension.

"Honey, are you sure you don't want me to drive?"

Lia wiped her hand across her cheek. "No, I'll be fine. Sorry, I know you must be terribly confused." She put the blinker on. "Let's just pull over at the bridge parking lot. I thought I wanted to walk, but I think I just really need some fresh air." She touched Gigi on the arm lightly. "And your listening ear."

Lia parked and Gigi waited until they were both standing outside, leaning on the car with the view of San Francisco and the Golden Gate Bridge in front of them. She'd never seen Lia quite like this before. She reached over to grab her friend's hand.

"Lia, what on earth is going on? You're really starting to scare me."

"I'm sorry."

"What happened at the doctor's appointment? Is Antonio alright?"

Lia took a deep breath in before she started to cry.

"Oh, honey, tell me what's happened. Please."

"Antonio has had a heart attack."

"What?" Gigi hugged Lia as she cried. "But he seems fine. Is the doctor sure about this?"

Lia nodded. "Yes, he did an EKG and a blood test. There's a lot more to be done—to find out the damage and the likelihood..."

"Okay, so is this something that you and Antonio are arguing about? I'm sorry. I don't understand what was happening between you two when you dropped him off."

Lia seemed to pull herself together enough to speak. "Yes, well of course the doctor wants to do some follow-up tests. They need to be able to assess the damage and get a good picture of everything. He really wanted to get started on this even today, but for sure over the next few days and—well, Antonio insists that he's well enough to fly today—that he can do the other tests in San Diego."

Gigi was quiet for a moment as she took everything in. She wanted to be supportive, yet objective—which is what she'd want from her friend if it were she going through the situation with Douglas.

"And did the doctor not think that was reasonable?"

Lia shook her head. "He said that he'd be happy to give us a referral, but that in all good conscience, he'd prefer that Antonio take the time to complete the tests while we're here."

"Okay. And you two know that you can stay here as long as you need to—in fact, Douglas and I don't need to be in any rush either. I know that everyone would understand."

"That's what I told Antonio. Oh, Gigi—I have no idea why he's being so stubborn about it all. I mean, it's not unusual that he wouldn't necessarily think the worst about a health situation, but I am surprised that he would let me get so upset about it—that he wouldn't at least respect my feelings about it when it's been upsetting me so much."

Gigi nodded. "Well, maybe he'll come around. I'm sure it's a lot to process, and having just heard the news this morning—it probably hasn't sunk in yet. I can't really believe it myself. And Lia, thank goodness he's okay."

"I know. I keep telling myself the same thing"

Gigi didn't miss the look that crossed Lia's face. It was a look of fear, and she didn't blame her friend for feeling that way.

Lia took another deep breath before she continued speaking. "And if he doesn't come around?"

Gigi put her arm around her friend. "Well, then we'll get him an appointment with a specialist in San Diego and see to it that we get the answers you need, won't we?"

Lia smiled. "Yes, I suppose there's no use arguing with him —of making things worse between us. I need to be thinking about any stress that he's under now too, and I certainly don't want to add to that. I guess I just want a clearer picture. I mean we need to know how bad things are, right?"

Gigi nodded. "Yes. We'll just have to get this train going forward as soon as we can."

Lia looked out toward the water. "Okay then. Do you still feel up for a little walk? Shall we go partway across the bridge? I think the exercise and fresh air would do me some good."

Gigi looked at the time on her phone. "Yes, I'd say we have about an hour before we should think about heading back to get ready for our flight. Do you want to phone Antonio?"

"Yes, I think that's a good idea. I'll just be a minute."

Gigi watched Lia walk a few steps to sit on an empty bench along the sidewalk that led to the bridge. How would Gigi react if it were she and Douglas going through this? She could easily see Douglas being as stubborn, and she felt great sympathy for her friend.

She could tell as she watched Lia that things were being patched up between the two—a stoic swipe of her hand across her cheek, a quick smile—both women knew the meaning of life being cut short, and those thoughts had to have entered the mind of her friend.

They'd all leave for the beach in a few hours, and everything was going to be just fine with Antonio.

"Are you ready?" Lia called over to her.

"Yep." Gigi started walking toward her—toward the bridge where she'd taken so many walks over what seemed like a lifetime ago. Yes, she would just hope, pray, and believe that everything was going to be just fine.

NINE

Blu looked over at Gigi and Douglas, who seemed to be just as uncomfortable as she and Chase were. They'd arrived, along with Lia and Antonio, about twenty minutes earlier. Antonio had given them and Isabella and Thomas what felt like a quick summary of what had transpired earlier that day, before he and Lia excused themselves to their room upstairs.

Blu squeezed Chase's hand under the table where the four now sat, feeling more than a little confused about what was going on.

"Gigi, is everything really going to be okay?"

Antonio had certainly seemed very matter-of-fact about the diagnosis he'd received, but Blu hadn't missed the worry that had been apparent on Lia's face.

Gigi shook her head. "I don't know. I sure hope so." She glanced quickly at Douglas before continuing. "Honestly, he's being stubborn—and it's driving Lia more than a bit crazy, as you can imagine."

Blu didn't miss the look that Douglas now gave his wife and the irritation that it seemed to cause her.

"Well, honey, it's true and you know it. We could have just stayed a few more days. He knows it was the right thing to do. You men..."

Douglas leaned over to kiss her on the cheek. "Darling, don't go lumping me into any sort of category that has you all bothered. And in Antonio's defense, I think it's possible that he's in a bit of shock. You know, it's not every day that you get news like that."

Chase nodded. "No, you're right. It's a hard pill to swallow, that's for sure. A buddy of mine recently passed away of a heart attack on the golf course—no warning, no previous problems—"

"Chase! Please!" Blu felt a lump rising in her throat.

"No, sorry, I didn't mean anything bad by it—just that Antonio's lucky, you know. He has a chance to do something about it, to figure out what's going on and hopefully lessen the likelihood of it reoccurring, right?"

"Well, I sure hope that's the case," said Gigi. "I don't really know what he's thinking. He's been pretty quiet ever since we left for the airport." She looked at Blu. "And Lia, of course, is upset—more upset than what she just let you see, but it's good that we're here now, that we're all together."

"That is good, yes."

Blu turned to where Lia stood in the doorway, her eyes red, her face slightly flushed.

"And I'm sorry that we just sort of dropped a bomb and left you all here like that."

Blu got up to walk across the kitchen and hug her friend, noticing that Isabella had been following right behind her. "You don't need to apologize for anything. I can only imagine how scared you must have been to get news like that." She pulled away enough to look her friend in the eyes. "And they're sure? That it really was a heart attack?"

Lia nodded, taking Isabella's hand as she led her over to a chair at the table. "Yes. The doctor seemed very confident after looking at the EKG results, and the blood test that we did do this morning confirmed it."

"It's going to be okay," said Isabella. "My grandpa is tough and healthy as a horse, and Lia—it could have been so much worse, right?"

Lia hugged Isabella to her. "Yes, you're right." She took a deep breath. "I think the whole thing just has us feeling stressed, but we have an appointment so that's good. It's not until Wednesday, but—well, I'm just going to do my best to keep an eye on that husband of mine, even if I do end up driving him crazy."

She laughed lightly but Blu could sense the truth behind her words. The appointment was still two days away, and Blu suspected that Lia wasn't going to have any peace of mind until they had more answers. She herself wouldn't if this were about Chase, so it was easy to understand.

Isabella laughed lightly. "Thus the fact that he's actually having a little rest right now."

"And probably not really resting," said Lia. "But we'll take what we can get, won't we?"

Isabella nodded and the two hugged again.

"Okay, so let's talk about something else. What's our plan for tonight and what can I help with? And also, where is that daughter of mine?"

"Chase is planning to grill—probably soon, actually—and you can help me with the salad and sides in a little while. And Gabby—she did call you, didn't she? Well, she told me that she had your permission to go to a party with Kylie. They have strict orders that curfew is ten tonight, but if you want her home, I can let Kylie know."

Lia was quiet for several seconds. "You know, I think I do want her here."

Blu could tell that Lia was trying to hold back tears. The emotional impact of the day was written all over her friend's face, despite what looked like a good attempt to keep it together. She reached her hand out to Lia's shoulder. "I'll call Kylie."

"No, let me text Gabby. Did they drive over?"

"No, they went with one of Kylie's friends and the plan is to take a taxi home. I know the neighborhood where they are and it all seemed pretty reasonable to me at the time."

"Oh, it's fine. I do vaguely remember Gabby asking me about going. I just think I've been in such a fog today that I spaced out or something. But I'll text her now. I'm not going to tell her anything over the phone, but I—I think she won't have a problem with it and—I don't know, I just want all my family together right now."

It was Blu's turn to lean down and give her friend a hug, thankful also that they could all be there for her now. Everything was always easier when the family was together, and Antonio's health scare was not going to be the exception.

TEN

Gabby tried not to look as uncomfortable as she felt. Why had she agreed to go to the party with Kylie and her friend, Whitney, anyway? It was clear to Gabby that she didn't belong there, in an apartment full of models and aspiring models-to-be.

Gabby did not fit in here—not at all. With her curvy—but vertically challenged—shape and distinctive Guatemalan dark features, she knew that she looked more like the women serving the guests food than the typical blond-haired-blue-eyed California type that she saw all around her.

She sighed and tried not to look too awkward as she took a drink of her soda and waited anxiously for Kylie to return from wherever she'd run off to—for just a second, she'd said.

Gabby wasn't used to attending parties—well, not like this one, anyway. Back home, she did go to parties, but there was never alcohol and there was always a parent not too far off. Kylie hadn't said anything to her—she didn't have to. Gabby knew at first glance that this was not like the parties she'd been to back home.

She spotted Kylie across the kitchen, her head thrown back, laughing at something the guy next to her seemed to be saying. Should she make her way over there? She suddenly didn't have a clue why she'd come. No, that wasn't entirely true. She did know why, and it had everything to do with spending time with Kylie, her best friend since as long as she could remember.

She sighed. She knew that their relationship had changed.

Kylie had changed. And Gabby wasn't at all sure if she wanted to be around this new version of her best friend.

She turned as she felt someone tap her on the back.

"Abby, come on. Come over here by us."

"It's Gabby," she said under her breath as she allowed Whitney to pull her into the kitchen.

Kylie hugged her after she'd entered the room, and Gabby didn't miss the smell of alcohol on her friend's breath.

"Gabby, do you want something in that?" Kylie nodded her head toward the plastic cup of soda in Gabby's hand.

"No, I'm fine, thanks." She forced a smile and thankfully felt her phone vibrating from inside the small purse over her shoulder. She reached in to pull her phone out and read the text from her mom.

Honey, can you come home, please? Dad and I just really miss you and I'd like you here.

Her initial reaction was one of relief. *Yes, please get me out of this place!*

But then, just like that, she remembered how her mom had sounded earlier on the phone—after her dad's doctor appointment. She'd said everything was fine, that they would talk to her about it all later, but she hadn't sounded fine. Why had she come to this stupid party anyway?

She wrote a quick reply to her mom and tucked her phone

back in her purse as she walked over to Kylie, now determined to speak to her.

"Kylie, sorry—I need to get home."

Kylie, Whitney, and the guy Kylie had been talking to all turned to look at her as if she'd just said that aliens had landed in the living room.

"Don't be silly, the party has only just started." Whitney laughed and tugged at Kylie's arm. "And this one is not going anywhere anytime soon."

The boy standing next to Kylie whispered something in her ear—something that Gabby instinctively felt was about her—and Kylie shook her head.

"No, just give us a second." Kylie reached for Gabby's hand and walked her to a quieter corner of the room. "Come on, Gabby, try to loosen up a little bit. I swear, you'll have more fun. And I won't tell your mom. Just have one drink."

Gabby willed herself not to cry. She felt like she wasn't in on some big secret all of a sudden, and it was the worst feeling in the world. She didn't want to be on the outside of anything when it came to Kylie, but suddenly she felt as if she hardly knew the person standing in front of her.

"Kylie, please." She wiped at the tears that she couldn't hold back. "Mom texted me. She wants to me to come home and I don't know—I don't know what happened with my dad today, so I think I should be there. You said if I wasn't having fun, we'd leave."

"But you haven't even tried, Gab."

"I'm going. Are you coming with me?"

Her voice sounded stronger than what she felt.

"Will you hate me if I stay?"

It was her best friend again, and Gabby didn't know why she felt sorry for her all of a sudden.

She hugged her. "No, no, of course I don't hate you. But I need to go."

"Okay. You know where the cabs are, yeah? Just down the street at the corner?"

"Yes. Yeah, I can manage."

"And you won't tell?"

Gabby bit her bottom lip. No, she wasn't a snitch. But she had the feeling that keeping Kylie's new secrets wasn't going to do her best friend any good.

She'd wait until later, then she'd talk to Kylie about everything—get her to understand how being around her like this had made her feel. She'd only ever known Kylie to be the most thoughtful and fun person in the room. She'd only ever known Kylie to be one of her biggest cheerleaders.

Gabby wanted to cry yet again for the thoughts she was having about her best friend, but somehow she managed to hold it together as she gave Kylie a quick hug.

"No, I won't tell, but Kylie?" She looked her friend in the eye, thankful that she didn't appear drunk or anything.

"Yeah?"

"You won't drink any more, will you? I don't know what I'd do if something ever happened to you and"—her gaze shifted around the room toward the other teens, who were obviously getting a little too wild and crazy—"just promise me you won't. And you'll be home by ten like we told your mom?"

Kylie laughed. "Don't be overly dramatic. And no. I won't let things get out of hand and I'll be home by curfew. Thanks, Gab."

"For what?"

"For not making a big deal of my wanting to stay. I promise we'll have lots more time to spend together." She grinned and managed one more quick hug before Whitney came up to pull her away again.

"I sure hope so."

Kylie whispered the words before she walked out the door.

ELEVEN

Kylie paused for just a moment when she saw Gabby walk out the door. But then Whitney was talking to her about the after party for a modeling shoot they were both booked for the next weekend. Kylie had never had as busy a social life as she'd had the last few months, and she was thankful that her parents did trust her enough to let her go out and do things with her new friends. And it was summer, after all.

She felt a pang of guilt, though—for the way that Gabby had looked when she'd told Kylie that she wanted to leave. As much as Kylie didn't want it to be true, the reality was that Gabby didn't really fit in there. Kylie didn't mean it in a mean way. She loved Gabby. She just wished that she would make more of an effort to fit in a little bit. Maybe she'd let Kylie do a makeover on her while they were in San Diego—just something to freshen up her look a bit.

"Here you go, babe."

Kylie smiled as she took the glass from Lance, the friend that Whitney had been dying to introduce her to. They'd be perfect together, she'd said, and Kylie did not dispute his good lucks or charm—so far. But then again, Kylie didn't have a lot of experience when it came to guys. And calling her babe? She wasn't so sure about that either.

She'd never really dated. In Italy, she and her friends tended to hang out in groups and she liked it that way, actually. It was something that she and Gabby had in common. She bit her lip as Gabby's words flashed through her mind. Did she know what she was doing? With the drinking and these parties? With these strangers who had somehow started to become her friends?

She took a very small drink as Lance watched her, then set the glass down on the counter. She definitely wouldn't have more than this to drink. The last thing she needed was her mom and dad becoming suspicious of anything she was doing while they were at the beach. That could put an end to her entire summer plans, and she was excited to be at the beach for the summer.

"Kylie, you've got to meet Vanessa. She's a new girl around town and rumor has it that she's starring in a new sitcom this fall. Come on." Whitney glared at Lance as he rolled his eyes. "What? Don't act like you weren't just into her a week ago."

"I wasn't. Well, I'd hardly say that one coffee date meant that I was into her." He laughed as Kylie raised an eyebrow. "I mean, she is pretty fabulous-looking, isn't she?"

Kylie wasn't sure why, but the conversation was making her feel uncomfortable—like they were talking about the poor girl behind her back, which they were, but it didn't seem all negative.

Before any of them could make a move, Vanessa had strolled up behind Lance, placing her arm around his waist.

"Fancy meeting you here, darling." She winked and Kylie felt her own face get warm as Vanessa proceeded to plant a big kiss on Lance right in front of them. "And who do we have here?"

Kylie was now definitely being scrutinized by this girl and she hated the way it made her feel, especially with both Whitney and Lance watching to see what her next move would be.

She stuck her hand out with the confidence that her father had taught her since she was very young.

"Hi, I'm Kylie. And you are?"

"Vanessa." She shook her hand and the handshake lasted just long enough for Kylie to notice her very well manicured fingers and several rings that were most certainly real jewels.

"Well, it's good to meet you, Vanessa."

"Likewise, and I see that you know the infamous Lance."

Lance moved quickly out of Vanessa's reach as she went to place her arm around him again. And Kylie couldn't help but smile brightly as he moved to stand closer to her than to this girl who seemed to have a need for all the attention available in the room.

"I'm not infamous. Not in the least." Lance smiled at Kylie and held her gaze for a second.

Vanessa turned toward Whitney. "Oh, anyway, I've got to tell you about this part. Let's move into the living room. The news hasn't officially been released yet."

Whitney followed her out of the kitchen and Kylie grinned at the look on Lance's face.

"What?"

"She's a real piece of work, isn't she?"

"Meaning she's the type of girl you go for?" Kylie took

another sip of the drink she'd clutched after Vanessa had made her feel so uncomfortable.

Lance reached out to take her hand. "No, not at all. You're the type of girl I go for."

Kylie felt her face go warm as she looked across the room. "You don't even know what type of girl I am."

"Well, I want to know. And I do know that I like what I see."

Her eyes went back to his and she tried to hold his gaze. She wasn't used to flirting and she definitely wasn't use to a guy being so direct with her.

"Well, I'm not so sure that you don't have something going with Ms. Vanessa over there." Kylie nodded toward where Vanessa and Whitney sat talking on one of the sofas. She'd seen Vanessa glancing their way more than a few times, so it was obvious that she'd not lost interest in what Lance was doing.

"Seriously. There's nothing going on, although she might like to think there is. We had one coffee date and I learned more than enough to know that there wouldn't be a second. She's harmless though. And Whitney is right, actually—about her being a good person in the business to know."

"So, in other words, not someone I'd want to get on the bad side of?" She could almost see the wheels turning in Lance's head.

"Oh, I probably shouldn't have said that to you, huh? Meaning, not really in my best interest to point that out." He laughed lightly.

"Nah, I'm okay. She doesn't scare me. Besides, I'm only here for a few months anyway." She took another sip of her drink, enjoying the little flirtation that they seemed to have going.

"Well then?" Lance held his hand out to her. "Shall we go for a little walk? Get some fresh air?"

Kylie grinned and took his hand. "That sounds like a great idea."

TWELVE

Jemma smiled as she watched Mateo helping the younger girls to get settled with their food at the kid's table. He and Nicolas had fit in so easily with their family. It was as if they'd always been a part of it. She looked at the time on her phone and then over to where Gabriela sat across from her.

Gabby had been noticeably upset after she'd returned home to have a chat with Lia and Antonio, and Jemma knew that it had taken a lot of reassurance to make her believe that her father was really going to be okay.

Jemma was more than a little annoyed by the fact that Kylie, for whatever ridiculous reason, had chosen to let Gabby come home from the party without her. Gabby hadn't said much about what had happened, just that Kylie hadn't been ready to leave and it had been fine with her to leave on her own.

"Are you alright, sweetie?" Rafael whispered the words close to Jemma's ear as he sat down next to her at the table.

She looked over at him. "Yes, I'm fine. I'm just a little annoyed with you-know-who."

Rafael looked quickly toward Blu. "Your mom will handle it."

"I know. I just hate to think that she wasn't looking out for Gabby." She was trying to whisper, but the question was obvious on Gabby's face as she looked at her from across the table.

"What?"

"Oh, we were just talking about Kylie. I don't like that she let you leave the party without her tonight—that she didn't come with you."

"Everything's fine, Jemma. Really." Gabby looked down at her plate as she spoke the words, and Jemma wasn't buying it.

"Well, what did you think about this party you guys were at?"

"Honey." Rafael nudged her under the table.

Jemma was instantly sorry. It wasn't right for her to question Gabby and especially not at the dinner table with everyone there.

Gabby seemed to be choosing her words carefully.

"The party was fine. I don't know. It wasn't my scene, but what do I know about fancy California parties, anyway?" Gabby laughed, but Jemma could feel how uncomfortable she was talking about it. She probably felt bad talking about Kylie, and it was wrong of Jemma to put her in that situation.

"Jemma?"

She looked over at Blu, who said:

"I'll talk to Kylie when she gets home."

Jemma nodded. It was really none of her business, but if she was being honest, she was feeling a little haunted by her past. On the one hand, it felt like a lifetime ago; on the other, it was only just yesterday that she'd been partying it up with a no-good guy on a motorcycle. She didn't ever want that lifestyle for Kylie. Her younger sister had too much going for her to let that happen.

"Jem? Earth to Jemma." Isabella laughed as she tried to get Jemma's attention.

"Sorry. What was that?"

"I was just asking what you thought about letting the girls sleep upstairs together again tonight. Arianna could not stop talking about how much fun she had last night, and they seemed to do pretty well with getting to bed."

Jemma laughed as she saw Chloe's attention immediately turn toward her mom from across the deck. She got out of her chair to run across to her where Jemma sat.

"Can we, Mom? We promise we'll be good." She grinned at Jemma.

"Yes, I think that's fine. As long as you girls promise not to stay up all night."

"Yay!" Chloe ran back to the smaller table.

"I love this—having the kids together here," said Isabella.

"Me too. It's so good for them and they obviously don't tire of each other's company." Jemma laughed.

"Speaking of..."

Jemma grinned at her friend. "Yes?"

"I'm hoping that you and I can grab a lunch or something out this week—maybe these handsome husbands of ours wouldn't mind holding down the fort with the kids." She looked at Thomas sitting next to her.

"Oh, I'm pretty sure that can be arranged," said Thomas, giving her a quick kiss on the lips.

"Sounds good to me," said Jemma, turning her attention to her food. "Chase, these steaks are delicious."

"They sure are," said Gigi. "And Lia, let's make that new pasta dish one night this week."

Jemma and the others waited for Lia to respond, as she seemed caught up in something Antonio was doing in the kitchen.

"Lia?" Gigi reached her hand over to her friend. "He's fine, honey."

Lia nodded. "Oh, I know. Sorry. What were you saying?"

Gigi and Lia put their heads together as they discussed some menu ideas for the week. But Jemma continued to watch Lia, noticing that she was definitely not herself. It would be much better for her once Antonio met with the doctor for the remainder of his tests, if for no other reason than peace of mind. Jemma could easily imagine feeling the same way if it were Rafael who'd had a health scare. She shivered at the thought as she watched him help their daughters with something across the deck.

Jemma couldn't imagine anything terrible happening to any of them. As she looked around the table at the faces of the people who were all so important to her, she knew how lucky they were that this health scare of Antonio's had been just that and not something that had taken him from them. She'd been lucky enough to be part of a family that was completely supportive and there for one another. It had always been that way for as long as she could remember. And now they all needed to rally around Lia and Antonio.

She glanced over at Gabby again, thinking that she really did need to have a talk with her sister. Whatever Blu or anyone else said, it wasn't like Kylie to be choosing a party or her friends over her family at all. Maybe she just needed to be reminded of that.

THIRTEEN

Isabella smiled as she watched Gigi laughing at something Douglas was whispering in her ear. They'd had a wonderful meal, complete with dessert and several bottles of their favorite California wine. The air was the perfect temperature and Chase had a good fire going in the fireplace outside, where the kids were taking turns roasting marshmallows.

"Well, he's definitely out like a light," said Thomas after checking on Samuel.

"It's the ocean air around here. It has a way of making children very sleepy."

"And grown-ups?" Thomas laughed as Isabella yawned.

She looked at the time on her watch. "Whoa, how is it ten o'clock already? I suppose we'd better start getting these girls to bed."

She didn't miss the look that Blu gave Chase when Isabella mentioned the time. She'd heard Kylie telling her mom that she'd be home by their required ten o'clock curfew, and it looked like she was already a few minutes late.

Jemma looked over at her. "It's definitely past their bedtime, and if we have any hope of them falling asleep before midnight..." She laughed.

Blu stood up from the table. "Jemma, you and Rafael sit. Enjoy your wine. I can get the kids down tonight—well, if Bella will come help me." She laughed.

Isabella stood up from the table. "That's a deal."

After some protests and one more marshmallow round, she and Blu managed to get the kids upstairs and into their pajamas. They sat in a quiet corner of the large rec room as the kids watched one short video, their eyes already closing as they lay in their sleeping bags.

She grinned as she looked at her daughter lying in her sleeping bag in between Chloe and Daisy. The twins had fought over who'd get to sleep next to Arianna, and Arianna, ever the diplomat, had plopped herself down right between them. She looked like an angel from where Isabella sat watching, her wavy dark hair fanned out around her head, the slightest of smiles on her sun-kissed face.

"I think they're about out," said Blu.

Isabella nodded. "I think you're right. Now, let's hope they'll actually sleep through the night."

"I think they will. They spent a lot of time playing at the beach today."

Isabella reached her hand out to cover Blu's. "Thanks so much for inviting us. We really love it—being at the beach, but mostly just being with everyone. It's funny how it never seems to be too much, you know."

Blu smiled. "I do know. That's how you know you're with family, huh? It's just all so easy, well—mostly easy." Blu glanced at her phone, which she'd carried up with her.

"Kylie?"

"Yep. Chase just texted me that she's not here yet." She looked at her phone again. "And she's now officially forty minutes past curfew." Blu sighed.

"I'm sure she'll be home any minute."

"Right, but Bella, it's really not like Kylie. I'm afraid we're going to have to make a few changes around here—nip it in the bud. I just don't know what's going on with that girl."

Isabella thought she saw a glimpse of something she wasn't used to seeing on Blu's face. Fear maybe. "She's a good girl. Maybe she's just caught up in the excitement of being here, seeing her new friends and all that."

"Maybe. Or maybe we've made a big mistake letting her start the modeling." Blu shook her head. "If that's the case, I should know better. I mean, I've been around that world for so long. There's a lot that comes with it for the models, and maybe I've given her too much credit in being able to handle it at her age. The last thing I want..." Blu looked down, and it seemed to Isabella like she was fighting back tears.

"Don't worry. It's not going to be the same—as what happened with Jemma."

Of course Isabella hadn't known Jemma or any of them back when Jemma had gone through her wild days. By the time Isabella had met her best friend, she'd been on the other side of that scary time in her life. But Isabella had heard all about it. Jemma had told her how close she'd been to a whole different way of life—a way of life that had nearly ended her life.

Blu wiped away a tear. "It's starting to kind of resemble that time, Bella. Honestly. Believe me, I've asked myself so many times how it had all started with Jemma. Especially lately. I don't want to miss anything, you know? I don't think I could go through that again and if I thought..."

Isabella leaned over to give Blu a hug as she continued.

"If I thought that's what was happening—especially because we're here—I'd pack up and leave tomorrow. It's not worth that. But I want to trust her because I know that's not who she is."

"Just talk to her, Blu. She'll listen to you. She always does. I'm sure everything will be fine, but if you need to make some hard decisions, I'll stand by you—we all will. Even if it means leaving this gorgeous place." Isabella laughed lightly.

"Well, even if we left, you all could certainly stay. And anyway, we have to get everything with Antonio sorted out, don't we? I don't think anyone wants him flying again without him having seen the doctor here."

"That's for sure. I hope Lia can handle two more days. Honestly, I don't think I've ever seen my grandmother this stressed out before." Isabella didn't miss the look on Blu's face. "You have, though, huh?"

It was another major event that had happened in the past and Isabella had been told all about it long ago. They'd all filled her in on every last detail about Arianna—about her birth mother and her final days with them. Isabella knew that it had been a very painful time for Lia.

"Lia has been through a lot, but she's a strong woman. And I don't think there's any reason at this point to think that your grandfather isn't going to be fine." Blu smiled. "And on that note, I'd say it's safe to turn off the kids' video and head back downstairs to join the others."

Isabella stood up. "Sounds good to me."

FOURTEEN

Lia smiled as she watched Antonio playing a game of chess with Mateo. The table had been cleared and they all were sitting at different spots around the deck enjoying the fire and the cool night air. Jemma laughed at something Rafael said, her head close to his where they sat by the fire. And Gigi and Douglas had just gone to the kitchen for something. Lia patted the spot next to her when she saw her daughter coming back outside.

"Gabby, come sit by me."

Gabby obliged scooting in close so that Lia could wrap her arms around her. She kissed the top of her daughter's head, taking in the scent of her fruity shampoo. It was hard to imagine her daughter so grown up.

At sixteen, almost seventeen, Gabriela had two years of high school left. In many ways—all of them sweet to Lia and Antonio—their daughter was still that affectionate little baby that they'd both fallen in love with at the orphanage so many years earlier. She was always quick to cuddle up to them, to let them hug and kiss her. She seemed to crave affection at times, something that used to worry them as parents, but her seeming lack of interest in boys thus far had put their minds at rest.

Gabby wrapped her arms around Lia. "I'm glad you're here."

"We missed you too—even in that short amount of time."

"Mom?"

"Yes, honey?"

"Is Dad really going to be okay? I mean, can you actually have a heart attack and then be okay after that?"

"Oh, honey, yes. Sure you can. You know how stubborn your father is. And he says he feels fine." She squeezed her just a bit tighter. "And don't you worry. We're going to get everything taken care of when we see the doctor this week. He comes with glowing referrals, so I have full confidence in that."

"But I know you're still worried. I can tell."

Lia couldn't see Gabriela's face as she spoke, but she could hear the concern in her daughter's voice. "Well, I mean, there's really not much I can do aside from trying to keep him pretty mellow. I'm not sure how much that helps, but it's definitely not the right time for him to be running at the beach or anything like that." She looked over to where he was still playing chess. "I'm sure he'll be fine, Gabby. You'll help me to keep him occupied for the next few days, won't you?"

"Yes, I can do that." Gabriela sighed. "Especially with Kylie so busy."

Lia felt a slight pang of sadness for her daughter. Of course they were old enough to work out their problems—it wasn't Lia's place to get in the way—but she hated to see her daughter feeling bad, and it was very rare that it would be because of something Kylie had done. Typically they were one another's biggest cheerleaders, so any kind of friction between the pair was out of the ordinary.

"Oh, honey, I'm sure things with Kylie will be fine. You two probably just need to have a nice chat, don't you think?"

"Oh, I don't know. To be honest, I'm not so sure that I like her new friends here. Tonight wasn't fun for me. I'm not going to do that again."

"Well, you don't have to go anywhere you don't want to, although it's also possible that maybe you just need to get to know the others a bit better. I'm sure they must be nice—for Kylie to be hanging around them."

"Well, you'd think so."

Lia had to smile, imagining that Gabriela was rolling her eyes as she spoke. "Anyway, the kids and all of us are happy to have you here, so if she's busy with her other friends, you'll still have a good time, honey."

"I know." Gabriela looked at her phone. "It's eleven o'clock."

"You're concerned about Kylie?"

Gabriela hadn't said much to Lia—about why Kylie hadn't come home with her—during their earlier conversation, but it had mainly centered on the news they'd shared with her about her father.

Gabriela turned her body so that she was facing Lia, and right away Lia could see the uncharacteristic signs of worry on her daughter's face.

"Yes, I'm concerned. Mom, she promised me."

"That she'd be home before now, you mean?"

"Yes, that she'd be home by curfew and that she'd stop—"

The silence around them was deafening even though there was still plenty of laughter and conversation going on with the others outside. Lia reached out to take Gabriela's hand. "Gabby. Honey, what? What was Kylie doing?"

Gabriela looked a bit like a deer caught in headlights. But she wasn't a teenager who lied to her parents. Even when she was very small, when caught in a little fib, she'd almost immediately burst into tears right before a confession. When Lia looked at her daughter now, she saw that same scared little face, but now it wasn't about Gabby's little white lie, it was about covering up for her best friend.

"Honey, you have to tell us—or at least you need to tell Blu —if there was something going on at the party that Kylie shouldn't be doing—especially if it could cause her any harm. But I know that you know that."

Gabriela nodded, biting her lower lip—a telltale sign that there were thoughts racing around in her head. "I don't really think she's not okay. I just—oh, I don't know. Why doesn't she just get here?"

"Honey? Do you want to have a conversation with Blu?"

They both looked up at the same time as Lia saw the lights of a car pulling up the driveway, followed by the slam of a door before the car turned around to go back down the hill.

Gabriela stood up and Lia immediately could sense the relief throughout her daughter's body. As she watched her walk into the house, she knew that it wasn't the end of the conversation. If it were Gabriela, Lia would want to know what was going on. Blu deserved that also, and Lia wouldn't keep anything like that from her friend—not when it involved her child. But she'd talk about it with the girls first—and encourage Kylie to have a conversation with her mother.

FIFTEEN

Gigi rolled over in bed, laughing lightly as she locked eyes with Douglas.

"What are you still doing in bed?"

Douglas was almost always up before her. Depending on the day, she'd find him already sitting at his computer or just getting ready for a morning run.

"It's only five o'clock, my darling." He winked as he reached out for her, pulling her close.

"Is it? Well then, I'm awake early, aren't I?" She gave him a quick kiss on the lips before laying her head down on his chest.

"It sounded a little tense last night—after Kylie got home—didn't it?"

His words were said quietly but Gigi's heart seemed to beat a little faster at the mention of the night before. She'd never heard Kylie argue with her parents the way that she had last night. It has been uncomfortable for everyone and they'd all gone to bed just after it began, giving the three the privacy that they'd obviously needed.

Gigi sighed. "Yes, it did. I hope everything is okay. Poor

Gabby looked like she didn't know what to do. I'm sure she feels a little bit caught in the middle. Lia told me that they'd been talking about Kylie and the evening just before she pulled up in the taxi. I got the feeling that Gabby had told her something. But honey—you don't think Kylie would be drinking or doing drugs, do you? She's such a good girl."

"Darling."

Douglas's tone was telling, like he didn't want to say what he was about to say.

"Well, she is!"

"Yes, she is a good girl—she always has been. But honey, she was mostly definitely not herself last night—not from what I witnessed. I think she just seemed a little tipsy."

Gigi moved away from him a little bit so that she could see his face. "Well, we've got to nip this in the bud, before anything gets out of hand."

"Honey, *we* aren't going to do anything—well, at least not until we're asked. I'm sure Blu and Chase have a handle on it."

"I hope you're right."

They didn't speak for several minutes, and Gigi guessed the same thoughts were in her husband's mind as her own. They both knew what it was like for things to get to another level quickly when it came to teenagers. They'd been there through much of it with Blu and Chase already when Jemma had had her issues. Gigi couldn't bear for them to go down that road again with Kylie.

Douglas kissed the top of her head and she felt him shift away from her on the bed.

"I guess I'll get up, maybe go for a beach run as soon as it's light. Why don't you go back to sleep for awhile, honey?"

Gigi sat up at the edge of the bed. "No, no more sleep for

me. I'm wide awake now—or I will be once I get some coffee in me. I'll go downstairs and get a pot going. You take your time."

"Okay. And Gigi?"

"Yes?"

"Try not to worry, okay? Let's not make a bigger deal out of what happened than what it is. She's a teenager. Teenagers go to parties where there's alcohol. Kylie does have a good head on her shoulders and a very big heart. Let's not forget that."

Gigi smiled as she pulled on her robe. "You're right. Of course, you're right."

As Gigi walked down the stairs, she could already smell that someone had beaten her to making the coffee. She entered the kitchen to see Chase at the small breakfast table with the newspaper spread out before him. He looked up at her as she entered the room.

"Morning, Gigi." He stood up, folding the paper as he did so. "Here, have a seat. Let me get you a coffee."

"Thanks, and good morning to you too."

Chase placed the mug down in front of her and took his seat opposite at the table.

"You're up very early, aren't you? Couldn't sleep?"

Gigi shook her head. "Not very well, no." She looked at him carefully before she continued. "I don't want to pry, but is everything okay? With Kylie?"

Chase sighed and then took a long sip of his coffee. "Yeah, that wasn't a very good way to end our nice evening, was it? Sorry about that."

"No need to apologize to me—or to any of us, for that

matter. Your kids—your family—is what's most important. And Blu seemed very upset."

Chase nodded. "Yes, it was upsetting. We've never really had to deal with anything like this before with Kylie, so it kinda feels like it's coming out of nowhere, and Blu and I..."

Gigi could tell that he was slightly uncomfortable.

"It's okay. Honestly, I don't mean to get in your business."

"No. Don't feel like that. If anyone has something to say about all this, it's you and Douglas. We certainly don't forget what you did for us—what you did for Jemma—when we needed help."

"We love you guys. We'll always be here for you."

Chase reached across the table to put his hand on Gigi's. "I know that. We both know that." He was quiet for a second as he looked out the window. "Blu and I seem to have a difference of opinion about how to handle this—how to handle Kylie. I'm sure she'll fill you in, but I'll just say that that daughter of mine can be very convincing."

"Ahh, okay. So, at least she's sorry then, I guess."

"Oh yes, she's sorry. She was saying all the right things and I don't want to make it seem like I don't believe her, but—"

"—But you're more inclined to ground her than Blu is?" Gigi smiled.

"Yes, exactly. I don't want her to get the idea that she's not going to be disciplined for drinking and missing her curfew. I mean, we just can't allow that."

Gigi nodded. "True. But it is the first time, I assume?"

"It is. That's the point Blu was making—that we need to trust her like we've always done—when she says that it won't happen again."

"And it won't."

Gigi and Chase looked over toward Blu as she made her way to the coffee pot.

Chase got up and walked across the room to kiss her on the cheek. "Good morning, love. Perfect timing as I'm leaving for my run. I'll leave you two ladies to enjoy your coffee."

"And me." Jemma laughed as she entered the room, pausing to kiss Blu on the cheek. "I want to enjoy some coffee with you too."

"Have a good run, honey," said Blu as she made her way over to where Gigi sat at the table.

Gigi could tell by the puffiness of Blu's eyes that she'd been crying. A good chat was definitely in order.

SIXTEEN

Blu sat down at the table across from Gigi, scooting over to make room for Jemma. She had hoped for a few moments alone with Chase before everyone else was awake, but it looked like that wasn't going to happen.

She felt exhausted. It had been a night of restless sleep once everything had died down and she'd gotten Kylie into her bed. The shock of seeing her daughter drunk still weighed heavily on her, but she was trying to push it aside until she could speak with Kylie again in the light of day.

"Are you okay, dear?" Gigi reached for her hand across the table.

"Mom? Are you going to tell us what happened?"

"Yeah, honey, just let me have a sip of my coffee, okay?" Blu laughed lightly and took a big drink from her mug, noticing the look that passed between Jemma and Gigi.

She hated it that they'd all been up the night before to witness Kylie coming home the way that she had. She hated it for Kylie because she knew that she'd be embarrassed about it, but also it made her second-guess everything that they'd been doing with their daughter. She knew that the others wouldn't judge them or their decisions—well, with the exception of Jemma, who'd been pretty vocal about not liking her sister's behavior lately—but at the same time, it felt like an added pressure that it had happened with everyone around.

"So?" Jemma seemed to be watching her carefully from where she sat next to her. "What's gotten into her? And please tell me that you've grounded her for at least the week."

"Jem, don't be like that. Just wait until the kids are older. You'll see that not everything is so black and white."

"So, what does that mean?"

"Honey..." Gigi caught Jemma's hand across the table. "Let's just listen for a minute, okay? I'm sure you're worried about your sister, but give your mom a chance to talk."

Blu smiled at Gigi, grateful for the support. "Thanks, Gigi. And honey, I know you're speaking from concern—I do get that. Look, Kylie knows what she did was wrong and she's sorry about it. And—"

"Yeah, well, she's sorry because she got caught—although coming home like that past curfew when she knows there's a house full of people isn't showing much intelligence, if you ask me."

"Jem, can I speak, please?" Blu was trying to be patient. She knew that Jemma would be all over her this morning.

"Sorry."

"So, I don't think it's so bad to give her another chance—to trust her when she says that it won't happen again. It's not like anything like this has happened before, and you both know what a good kid she is. I think she deserves the benefit of the doubt with this. And I—I believe her—that she's sorry."

"I'm sure she is," said Gigi. "I think that makes sense." She looked at Jemma. "And sweetie, I'm sure you're thinking about everything that happened here when you were a teen. It's understandable that you'd be upset about it—that you wouldn't want that for your sister."

Jemma nodded. "Exactly. It just scares me a little bit. I know what it can be like—the peer pressure, hanging around older kids who don't have the same rules—it's easy to get swept up in all that when you're sixteen. And add to that all the modeling stuff—well, I just think she's been thrust into an environment here that we need to keep a close eye on." She squeezed Blu's hand. "Can we agree on that at least?"

"Yes, honey, I do agree with you. Kylie has a show she needs to do on Friday night, but she's promised that she'll be around all week. I might still have a chat with her—about Gabby—I know her feelings were really hurt last night. I think it's important that Kylie knows that, and I'm not so sure how vocal Gabby will be about it."

"I think Gabby might surprise you," said Gigi. "She's pretty open—well, at least with her mom. But who knows? I know that she thinks the world of Kylie and their friendship. Those two are as tight as sisters themselves, so I'm sure they can work it out."

Jemma was quiet.

Blu leaned over to hug her. "You okay?"

"I'm sorry I've been so wigged out about all this. I know it's not really my business. And I guess it's possible that I could be blowing it out of proportion." She stopped talking, as she seemed to need to gather her sudden emotions.

"Oh, honey. Don't cry." Blu used her finger to wipe the tears that had appeared on Jemma's face. "Kylie's going to be just fine. Don't worry about it. Look, I promise you that nothing is going to get out of hand. We'll even ground her for the entire summer if she messes up again."

Jemma laughed. "Promise?"

Blu reached down to squeeze her hand. "I promise."

And she knew in that moment that it was a promise she had to keep.

Life was too fragile and sometimes children needed their parents to make tough decisions for them. Jemma had already taught Blu that lesson long ago.

SEVENTEEN

Kylie lay in her bed for a full ten minutes trying to remember what had happened the night before. She could vaguely recall Lance sending her home in the taxi, but she definitely remembered that her parents—and everyone else in the house—had been there to greet her when she'd gotten in. And she'd missed her curfew again!

She tried to remember when her second—and last—drink had turned into several more. There were memories of Whitney mixing some concoction in the kitchen and also memories of Lance kissing her. She smiled at the thought. She'd not been kissed by very many boys and, even though she wasn't sure how she felt about Lance, she didn't mind his kisses, that's for sure.

Gabby.

She frowned trying to remember what had happened when Gabby left. Was she going to be mad at her? She'd make it up to her today. Maybe the two of them could go shopping or something.

Wait! Was she grounded?

Her dad had definitely wanted to ground her. She'd never

seen him so angry before. But somehow she'd managed to keep it together enough to convince them—well, to convince her mom—that she wasn't going to let it happen again. She wouldn't be that stupid.

She had another party to go to on Friday after the photo shoot, but she'd try to hang around the beach house most of the week. Her parents would like that. It would keep them happy, and it wasn't like Kylie didn't love her family. Of course she did. But something about California made her want to be out and about more. She didn't want to feel like she was missing something with her new friends.

She heard a quiet knock on her door. Ugh. She certainly wasn't ready to talk to either of her parents yet. She could pretend to be asleep for a while longer. Her head was aching anyway.

There was another knock, followed by the quiet calling of her name.

She smiled. "Come in, Gabby."

Gabby entered the room and Kylie sat up when she saw the cup of coffee that she was handing her.

"Oh my gosh, I love you. Thanks, Gab." She scooted over in the bed so Gabby could sit down next to her.

"I figured maybe you could use it." She smiled. "Are you okay?"

Kylie nodded. "Yeah, I have a bit of a headache—oh, and I vaguely remember throwing up during the night—but other than that..." She looked at her friend, suddenly feeling an intense pang of guilt. They'd been best friends for so many years —through thick and thin, they'd always been there for one another. She didn't like the distance that she was starting to feel between them but she wasn't entirely sure how to fix it either.

"Sorry to hear about the puking. I know how much you hate that."

Kylie took a big drink of her coffee. "Are you mad at me? I'm really sorry for last night. I probably should have just come home with you."

Gabby nodded. "Well, I think it would have ended up better for you too. Did you get in bad trouble?"

"No, I actually somehow think I managed to not be grounded. That's all my mom. Dad was pretty livid, really—set to ground me for the rest of the summer, I think."

"Kylie?"

"Yeah?"

"Have you done that before? Gotten drunk? Because I sure haven't and—well, you've never told me anything, so..."

Kylie shrugged. "No—well, not like that anyway. I don't know. It feels different here, Gabby. It's a little harder to fit in than back home. Whitney and all her friends—well, it's pretty much the norm for them." She laughed at the look on Gabby's face. "Not a fan of Whitney?"

"She kept calling me by the wrong name. And—I don't know." Gabby shrugged.

"What? Just say it."

"Well, you just seemed different around them. It made me feel sad last night."

Kylie knew her friend well and she could tell that Gabby was holding back tears. She reached out to grab her hand. "I'm sorry. I'm not different. And I think maybe you'd like Whitney and the others if you hung around them a bit more. They're not so different from us.

Gabby was shaking her head. "No, I'm not really interested in hanging around with Whitney. Sorry. But you do what you have to do. I just hope that we can spend at least a little time together while we're here. The beach and being here with everyone is great and everything, but it was mostly hanging out with you here that I was looking forward to."

"Let's go for breakfast together, okay? I know the cutest little place and I can be ready in ten minutes." Kylie suddenly remembered the text she'd gotten from Gabby the night before —about something that had happened with her dad. "Oh, wait! Tell me what happened last night with your parents. I did get your text. Sorry."

Gabby sat back down on the bed and filled her in about the news that her mom and dad had gotten while they were in San Francisco. Even talking about it with her best friend made her feel better—less scared. She'd known that it would.

"Wow! I'm so glad he's okay. He is going to be okay, isn't he?"

Kylie couldn't imagine anything ever happening to her own father. If she were in her friend's position, she'd be worried, that's for sure.

"Well, they have an appointment tomorrow and that's when they're going to run a bunch of tests and—"

Gabby was interrupted by the sound of Kylie's stomach growling loudly.

Kylie laughed. "Hold that thought. Let's talk about this over food. I'm starving!"

Gabby grinned. "Deal! I'll go get ready."

"Me too." Kylie reached for her phone when it buzzed with an incoming text as Gabby left the room.

EIGHTEEN

Jemma laughed at Chloe and Daisy as they paraded around in front of her wearing her heels. "You girls be careful now, we don't want any twisted ankles."

"Darling, we're always so careful," said Chloe in a too-cute-for-words accent that she'd been perfecting over the past few weeks.

"Mother, darling?" Daisy tried to copy her sister, and Chloe nodded her head in encouragement.

"Yes, darling?" Jemma was happy to play along. She loved watching the girls play make-believe and never tired of watching their creativity unfold.

"Would you like to join us for our tea party?"

"Oh yes, Mother. Please do give us your RSPP soon," said Daisy.

Jemma laughed. "RSVP. And yes, I will happily attend. How shall I dress?"

Daisy ran over to whisper into her sister's ear and Chloe nodded.

"Summer casual, Mommy."

"Got it! And are you inviting anyone else to this party of yours?"

"Ari, of course, and maybe Gabby and Kylie. Oh, Chloe, are the boys invited?"

Chloe spent a full twenty seconds deep in thought before responding. "Nope! Only girls today!"

Jemma nodded. "Okay, as long as you don't exclude them every time."

"Mommy, the boys are busy with Daddy anyway," said Chloe.

"That's right."

Rafael had taken Mateo and Nicolas out for breakfast earlier. Jemma thought it was nice for them to have some father-son bonding time, so she always encouraged it when it made sense.

"Where is Ari?" Daisy asked.

"That's a good question. Hey, I have an idea."

"What?" the twins asked in unison, eager to hear what she would suggest.

"Would you like to make some cookies for your tea party?"

"Yes!"

"Alright then, why don't you two go ask Arianna if she wants to join us? And get dressed too while you're at it. I'll meet you in the kitchen in ten minutes."

"It's a deal, Mommy!" Chloe said, sticking her hand out.

"Mommy, you have the best ideas!" Daisy threw her arms around Jemma's neck. "You're the best mommy ever!"

Jemma reached out to pull them both close, one in each arm, as she took turns kissing their faces while they giggled.

"And you are the best daughters ever! I will not be trading

you in any time soon." She laughed as they scampered away from her.

"Okay, see you in the kitchen!" Chloe called over her shoulder.

Jemma smiled as she got up from the floor to go downstairs. She heard music playing from Gabby's room as she neared it and stopped outside of the slightly open door to knock, before pushing it the rest of the way open.

"Hey, Gabby, wanna come help us—hey, what's wrong?" She made her way quickly to the edge of the bed to take Gabby's hand when she saw that she was crying. She waited a few seconds for her to compose herself, handing her a tissue from the bedside table. "Are you okay?"

Gabby nodded and took a deep breath, her tears seemingly stopped for the moment. "Yeah, I'll be okay."

"Do you wanna talk about it? Did Kylie do something?" As soon as the question was out of her mouth, Jemma thought how weird it sounded. She never would have thought there'd be a time when she'd be asking Gabby if it was Kylie that was making her feel bad.

"Oh, I don't know. I'm probably making too big a deal out of it."

"I haven't even seen her yet this morning. Have you?"

"Yeah, we had a really nice chat earlier, actually. We were going to go out for breakfast—just she and I—and then while I was getting ready Whitney texted her or something."

"Oh." Jemma did not like whatever was happening with Kylie and these new friends of hers. She'd never known her younger sister to be hurtful or non-inclusive when it came to others, especially when it came to Gabby. "Honey, did she not invite you to go along?"

"No. No, she did invite me, but I dunno." Gabby wiped away a few more tears. "I was kinda looking forward to it being just us, you know? And to be honest, I don't really like Whitney. I just don't see what Kylie sees in her. She's definitely not like Kylie's friends back home, that's for sure."

Jemma didn't really know what she could say to make Gabby feel better. She needed to talk to her sister—knock some sense into the girl. She was heartbroken for Gabby, but it was something the two of them needed to work out. And they would work it out. She was sure of that.

"Well, then I guess it's our luck, because I've got two little girls—probably three with Arianna—who are planning a special tea party this morning, and your name was on that guest list right at the top."

Gabby smiled. "Well, I'm sure that will be a fun time."

"And we're just going down to make cookies, actually. Rumor has it that Gigi picked up all the ingredients we could ever want to make any of our favorites so we're planning for a little baking extravaganza. And you *are* the baker in the family."

"Am I now? Who told you that?"

"I've heard your father mention it." Jemma grinned, happy that Gabby's mood seemed to have lifted a bit. "So what do you say? Can I get your help in the kitchen?"

"Sure. Let me just put my sweats back on—get comfy." She leaned over to hug Jemma. "Thanks, Jemma."

Jemma squeezed her back. "No need to thank me. I just don't want you being sad. Don't worry. It will all work out."

Gabby nodded. "So, tell the girls I'll be down in a few minutes."

"Will do, and we won't start without you."

NINETEEN

Gabby was thankful for Jemma—and the kids. If it weren't for them being there right now, for sure she'd be feeling depressed. She'd been happy when they found out that they were going to spend the summer at the beach house—who wouldn't be? All her friends back home in Italy thought she was so lucky to be living in California for the summer. And she knew that she was too. But right now, she'd give anything for her and Kylie to be chilling out back at the vineyard—for things to be the way they used to be.

She cringed as she thought about the conversation they'd had only minutes before. Gabby had been so happy when Kylie had suggested going to breakfast together. It seemed like she'd really felt bad for what had happened the night before.

So she'd just been taken aback when all of a sudden everything had changed—when Kylie had come bounding into her room with a big grin on her face as if Gabby would be happy to join her and Whitney at some fancy new tea shop that she said Kylie would just adore.

Did Kylie even drink tea?

Gabby didn't even take a moment to think about it—she'd just reacted, shouting at Kylie to just go on without her—that she had no interest in going anywhere with that stupid girl who couldn't even remember her name. Gabby couldn't remember ever shouting at Kylie like that, and now the tears threatened again just thinking about it.

She finished changing clothes and then sat back on the bed with her phone in her hand. She certainly didn't want Kylie mad at her. And things had felt so much better between them earlier that morning. She sighed as she pulled up her text app.

Sorry for yelling at you earlier. Hope you're not mad.

She waited for a full minute, willing Kylie to text her right back and when she didn't, she tried not to imagine her and Whitney laughing about it. Wow! That was a horrible thought, and where did it come from? Kylie wasn't like that. Gabby knew that deep down, they'd always be best friends—that Kylie would always have her back.

At least she wanted to believe that still.

Gabby could hear the girls before she was even close to the kitchen, their voices raised, and the sound of chairs being dragged across the floor, no doubt so that each could take her position in front of some counter space.

"Gabby! Come by me, please," Arianna called out.

"No, I want Gabby to stand by me!" said Chloe.

Gabby grinned. "I'll be right there and I can stand by each of you. We'll take turns. You girls just watch what you're doing there." She laughed as bits of the flour mixture spilled over Arianna's bowl.

"Oh, no!" Arianna screamed and Gigi came rushing up behind her.

"Ari, it's fine." Gigi laughed too and then put the little blob of dough right back into the bowl.

Gigi winked at Gabby. "Jemma's just gone to the store down the road, so I think I can use your help, just as soon as you're able."

Gabby nodded. "Okay, let me just go give my dad a hug."

She'd seen her parents sitting quietly at the breakfast table when she'd walked in.

She kissed Lia on the cheek and then threw her arms around Antonio. "Morning, Daddy."

"Morning, sweetheart. I hear you girls are going to bake us something delicious."

"That we are." She looked at her father carefully. "Dad?"

"Yes, daughter dear."

"Are you feeling okay?"

She didn't miss the look that passed between her parents.

"Is something wrong?"

"No, nothing's wrong, honey."

"Then why are you two giving each other a look?"

Lia reached out to take her daughter's hand. "Your dad's just feeling a little under the weather, that's all."

"I'm sure it's nothing. Maybe a bug," said Antonio.

"And tomorrow you're going to the doctor, right?"

"Yep." Antonio nodded his head.

"Good, and I'm going with you guys."

"Honey, that's not necessary. You'll stay here, hang out with Kylie..." Antonio leaned over and kissed her nose. "What? Now you're the one making the funny faces."

"Where is Kylie? Still in bed?" said Lia.

Gabby sighed. "Maybe I'll talk about it with you later, okay, Mom? Right now I think I'd better get over there and help Gigi with the kids—the little cookie monsters."

They all laughed as Gabby made her way back over to where Gigi had the girls placing their little blobs of cookie batter on the baking sheets in front of them.

Gabby tried not to look at her phone too many times over the next hour while she was busy with the girls baking cookies. When thirty minutes had gone by without a reply, she'd texted Kylie once more, just telling her that she really hoped they could hang out together a little later that day—maybe go see a movie or something.

But now as she sat quietly with the girls at the table, she felt certain that Kylie was indeed angry with her.

"Do I have any takers for the beach?" Isabella entered the kitchen followed by Thomas, who seemed to be carrying every possible beach toy that he could get his hands on.

"What do you think, girls? Shall we go play in the sand for a bit while the cookies cool?" said Jemma.

"Yes!"

"Okay, run get your suits on. I'm going to get this kitchen cleaned up quick."

"Jemma, don't worry about that." Lia got up from the table. "I'll help Gigi with it. We're going to get started prepping some food for lunch anyway. You all go on."

Antonio stood up from the table. "I think I'll go too—get a little fresh air."

"Oh, honey, I don't think that's a good idea—"

"Lia, I'm fine. Please."

Gabby could hardly remember a time when her father had

spoken harshly to her mom, but he sounded more than a bit annoyed.

Gabby walked over to take his hand, looking quickly at Lia, then back at her father. "I'll go with you—for some good father-daughter bonding time, right, Dad?"

Antonio kissed her on the forehead. "Okay, honey."

TWENTY

Isabella smiled as Thomas reached out to take her hand.

Jemma, Gabby, and Antonio were not too far ahead of them and they seemed to be doing a good job of keeping the children all together. Samuel was down for a nap, with Gigi's ear tuned in to the monitor.

The air was the perfect temperature and Isabella thought that she could listen to the sound of crashing waves every day of her life and not get tired of it. There was something about being near the ocean that inspired her. The rolling hills of Tuscany did also, but it was different being near the water. For the first time since Samuel had been born, Isabella was starting to have a frenzy of new book ideas brewing in her brain and it excited her.

"What's that smile for?" Thomas grinned at her.

Isabella laughed lightly. "I'm just happy." She stopped and kissed him on the lips when he stopped with her. "And I'm a very lucky wife and mother."

Thomas got that look in his eyes that made her heart beat

faster. It always surprised her—that he could make her feel so adored by just one look.

"I'm the lucky one." He tugged her forward with him as they followed after the others. "And yes, it really is wonderful being here. It's so good for the kids—being outside, being all together like this."

"I agree. I'm glad we have so much time left—and that you're not bored."

"Nah. I could never be bored with you—but you know that." He was looking at her intently again. "And what about you? Have you been giving any thought to when you might start writing again?"

It was so like Thomas to be this in sync with her—as if he were able to read her mind.

"Funny you should mention that, actually. No, I'm definitely not bored. Our kids keep me too busy for that, but it is nice having so many helping hands around while we're here. And I have been jotting down a lot of ideas that I'm feeling anxious to get started with."

"Well, I'd say that the beach house would be a pretty good writing spot."

"Daddy?"

Before Isabella could respond, Arianna was tugging on Thomas's shirt.

Thomas bent down to take his daughter's hand. "Yes?"

"Will you help me and Chloe and Daisy build the biggest sand castle? Please, Daddy?"

"The biggest in the whole wide world?"

"Daddy!"

Isabella and Thomas both laughed as their daughter stopped to stand with her hands on her hips—something she loved to do when she was feeling exasperated.

"What, honey? Not the biggest sand castle in the world then, I take it?"

"No, that's silly. We want to build a castle bigger than Nicolas's and Mateo's. See?"

She pointed to where it looked like the boys already had a good start on their masterpiece. It also looked like they had a partner in Antonio, who was making his way back from the water with a full bucket.

Antonio grinned when he saw Arianna's expression. "Don't worry, Ari, I'll get water for you girls too."

"Thanks, Grandpa! Come on, Daddy!"

Thomas and Arianna ran off and Isabella grinned at Jemma, who was busy spreading some blankets out on the sand.

"Oh, that looks amazing. May I?"

"But of course." Jemma grinned up at her. "I say, we mark out our territory while everyone else is busy."

"Where is Rafael, by the way?" Isabella sat down on the blanket next to her friend. "I've not seen him all morning."

"Would you believe that Chase got him out on the golf course this morning?"

"Wow! Gonna give it another try, huh?"

It was a standing joke that Rafael found the game a little too quiet for his liking. He was more a friendly game of basketball or soccer kind of guy. Isabella didn't blame him, because Thomas wasn't really into golf either.

Jemma laughed. "Yeah, well, he does like spending time with Chase, so I guess it seemed like a good idea—although he's probably going to be exhausted after such a busy morning. First the boys out for an early breakfast, then a big golfing day."

Isabella looked over to where Gabby was helping the girls to shape their sand castle. "Jem, where's Kylie, by the way? I don't think I've seen her all morning. I hope she didn't get into too much trouble from last night."

Jemma rolled her eyes. "Please. She could stand to be grounded right now, as far as I'm concerned." She lowered her voice just a bit. "I found Gabby crying earlier—because Kylie had bailed on plans that she'd already made with her."

"Ouch. Really? That doesn't sound like her at all."

Gabby hadn't said anything about it during the entire morning that she'd spent with the kids, but Isabella did notice now that she seemed more quiet than normal.

"Yeah, well, it seems that angelic sister of mine has turned into a rotten teenager after all."

Jemma laughed, but Isabella could sense her genuine annoyance.

"Well, let's not get too crazy. I'm sure the novelty of being here will wear off a bit. Maybe she's just anxious to get to know the other girls that she's modeling with while she's here. I can imagine that would put a little bit of pressure on a kid."

"I'm sure. I just hope she figures it out before she manages to get grounded for the entire summer—not to mention having her behavior causing a rift between her and Gabby."

"Mommy!"

Arianna's loud shout caused both Isabella and Jemma to jump to their feet. As if in slow motion, Isabella saw Thomas drop the shovel he was holding to sprint toward her grandfather, who lay on the sand next to a crying Arianna.

"Jemma, dial 9-1-1! Iz, run up to the house to meet the ambulance and tell Lia!"

Isabella stood for one frozen moment, as she watched her husband begin doing CPR on her grandfather.

"Iz, go!"

TWENTY-ONE

Lia watched the others as they made their way across the sand in front of the beach house. Antonio had been quiet that morning —more quiet than normal—and Lia couldn't shake the feeling that he wasn't being completely honest with her about how he was feeling.

She smiled as she saw Gabby walking beside him, her hand in his, laughing as she looked up at him. Where had the time gone? Gabby was growing into a lovely young woman, and Lia knew how fast the time would go over the next few years. It was so important to her that they have good quality time together. She sighed as she looked again at her husband in the distance now. She knew it was important to Antonio too.

"Alright then. Shall I get the pasta going?" said Gigi. "Lia?"

"What? Sorry. Oh, I meant to help you with that clean-up, Gigi."

"Don't worry about it. Jemma had it mostly done anyway," said Blu.

"We'll just focus on lunch. I've sent Douglas to the market to pick up a few things for a salad," said Gigi.

"Do you think Antonio is okay out there?" Lia had to mention it to her friends if she had any hope of not obsessing about the thought that she should go out there by him.

Gigi grabbed her in a hug. "Honey, I think he's fine, but go on if you want to. I'm sure Blu and I can handle lunch."

Lia wanted to go to him. But as she thought about it, she felt that Antonio would be irritated with her. She looked out the window again where she could see him carrying what looked like a full bucket of water back from the ocean, Arianna dancing next to him in the sand.

He was fine. Everything was going to be fine. They'd go to the doctor the next morning, Antonio would have the tests that he needed and he'd be cleared with a clean bill of health. He believed that, so why couldn't she? She almost felt like it was a betrayal of her husband to have any thoughts contrary to those that didn't include perfect health.

She looked back at Gigi and Blu, both waiting for her response. "No. No, I'm sure he's fine, and look how much fun he seems to be having with the kids. I'll get the bread going." She'd focus on the task at hand. "Where are Chase and Kylie, by the way? I don't think I've seen either of them this morning."

Blu smiled. "Chase somehow talked Rafael into playing golf with him this morning. And Kylie? That's a good question. I thought she was here, actually."

Lia noticed that Blu looked more annoyed than curious as to where Kylie might be.

"Gabby mentioned earlier that she'd gone out to breakfast with some of her new friends," said Gigi.

"Oh, yeah?"

"I take it she didn't say anything to you?" said Lia.

"No, she did not, and considering what happened last

night, I'm not particularly happy that she thinks she can just go taking off whenever she feels like it, especially when Gabby is here."

"I probably should stay out of it, but..." Lia hadn't really had a chance to talk to Gabby, but she knew that something had happened earlier that morning—before she came downstairs to bake cookies with the girls.

"What? Did she do something to hurt Gabby's feelings again?"

Lia nodded. "I think so, but you know, it's possible that Gabby is being super sensitive also. I'm sure we should just let the girls work it out for themselves, don't you think?"

"Well, you may be right but I swear, I don't know what's gotten into that girl." Blu walked over to pick her phone up from the table, pulling up a number and holding it to her ear as she left a message for Kylie to call her right away.

Lia clapped her hands together, ready to get her mind on food and off of anything negative. She'd definitely have a talk with Gabby later—make sure that she was really doing okay after whatever had taken place that morning, but for now, they'd cook. Cooking always made Lia feel better.

"Okay, well, let's get this food going. I've got the bread dough rising and it should be ready to go into the oven. Gigi, that sauce you have going smells delicious. Blu, if you wouldn't mind cutting up some vegetables, we can toss the rest of the salad together when Douglas gets back."

They worked on their individual tasks for a good thirty minutes, Lia enjoying the camaraderie she always felt while cooking with any of her family in the kitchen. It was easily one of her favorite things to do when they were all together, and the others seemed to like it too.

"Yum! Everything smells so good. I'm suddenly starving," said Gigi as she tasted the sauce for about the tenth time, causing Lia to laugh at her.

"I know. I am too. Let me get the bread out and then we can gather the troops," said Lia. "Let's eat outside, yes?"

"Sounds good to me," said Gigi as she poured her sauce over the huge bowl of pasta on the counter.

"I'll start setting the table." Blu walked across the kitchen to start pulling out dishes and silverware.

"Lia! Lia!"

Lia dropped the hot pan she was holding as she heard first Isabella's screams, followed by the sirens coming up the driveway. In one motion, she ran across the room, out the kitchen door to the deck and down the stairs to the beach, where she could see the commotion in the distance.

Please, God—I'll do anything—Please let him be okay.

TWENTY-TWO

Lia tried to see Antonio from where she sat in the front of the ambulance. She'd tried desperately to hold his hand—to sit next to him as they worked to get him stabilized. But there'd been too much commotion—too much that he needed. The driver had shouted to her that she had to let them help her husband— that she'd have to ride up front with him, but that Antonio was in good hands.

It had all happened so fast. One minute she'd been in the kitchen thinking about calling the others for lunch, the next, she'd heard the piercing scream of her granddaughter. And then the ambulance was there and they were all running to where her husband lay on the sand, not breathing—at least it had looked to her as if he wasn't breathing as the paramedics took over from Thomas.

Thank God for Thomas.

Lia wiped a tear away as she thought she saw Antonio's eyes flutter open where he lay in the back of the speeding ambulance. Yes, thank God for Thomas. She'd heard the men tell him that he'd done a fine job—that he'd probably saved Antonio's life.

Bella. What had Bella told her?

Blu was driving them—Bella and Gabby. They'd be with her while she waited. And Gigi and Douglas were on their way too. She wouldn't be alone. It was good, because her thoughts were all jumbled and she wasn't sure how to handle any of this.

What do you do when your husband is having a heart attack?

"Your husband is in good hands, ma'am. And the nearest hospital is one of the best." The driver didn't take his eyes off the road for one second as he spoke, diligent in his need for safety and with the utmost alertness as they carefully drove through intersections with sirens blaring. "We're only about two blocks away now."

She was grateful for the update. "Thank you. I think he's awake—at least I think his eyes are open now."

Lia tried to focus on her breathing. She'd be no good to him when they arrived if she was too wound up. Antonio needed her to be calm. He'd be stoic, as normal, but Lia thought about how terrified he must have been—and in front of the children. He wouldn't like that it happened in front of them.

She took one more big breath as the ambulance slid into a spot in front of the big emergency room doors. There were guys in scrubs just outside—waiting to take the patient.

As soon as they stopped, she threw open her door and ran straight for the back as Antonio was brought out on the stretcher. She reached to touch his hand as she heard the men relaying information.

Cardiac arrest—CPR—stable now. She let those words sink in. He was stable. Antonio was not going to die—not today, anyway. He'd been in cardiac arrest, but then Thomas had given CPR and now her beloved husband was stable.

She couldn't stop the tears. She tried to hold them in, but everything was a blur.

"Please, please. Can I just see him for a moment?" she begged the ones in charge, and then rushed forward again as she saw them nod first to one another and then to her.

"For one second, ma'am."

She nodded and took his hand. She wouldn't feel better—she wouldn't believe he was going to be okay—until she could look him in the eyes. She leaned down to first kiss him on the lips lightly, then she pulled away, but not too far.

"Sorry, babe."

He smiled ever so slightly and she smiled back at him. She knew what he meant without another word spoken. He should have listened to her. They should not have left San Francisco. But there was no time for blame now. She wasn't interested in that in the least as she smiled back at him.

"You don't worry about me, honey. You're going to be okay, you hear me? You just focus on being okay." She squeezed his hand one last time before the crew rushed him away and a woman appeared next to her, taking her gently by the arm.

"Please, come with me. We have a few papers for you to fill out and then we can get you settled in a private waiting room. You've got some people waiting for you inside. I'm sure they can help you with whatever you need."

How had the others gotten there so quickly?

Lia wasn't sure exactly what shock looked like, but it crossed her fuzzy mind that she wasn't thinking clearly. She looked down the hall and when she did, she saw Gigi and

Douglas. They saw her too and in seconds Gigi was at her side with her arm around her waist, pulling Lia to her for a hug.

Lia felt her whole body go limp as the sobs came. She let the two of them walk her to a chair, and she was grateful to see that Douglas had the clipboard with the papers—the papers she needed to look at. How did people function alone at times like this? How did people function when a loved one died in this situation?

She shook her head quickly as if she could banish the thought she'd just had. Antonio was not going to die. She'd heard the men say that he was stable. Stable was good.

"Honey, he's going to be okay," said Gigi.

Lia nodded.

"Lia, I can fill this out for you. Do you happen to have your insurance information on you?" Douglas asked. "If not, I'm sure we can get it later."

"Yes. Yes, I should have it—in my purse. Where is my purse?"

"Here you go. Right here."

Somehow Gigi was holding her purse. Lia must have set it down somewhere.

Lia stood up. Antonio's face as he'd looked up at her from the stretcher was suddenly all she could see in her thoughts. "I should go be with Antonio, shouldn't I?"

Douglas gently guided her back to her chair. "The doctor will be out soon, I'm sure. We need to wait here right now. I'm sure you'll be able to go back there by him before long."

Yes, she needed to be with Antonio.

She tried to focus on the words Douglas was saying to her. She could trust him. She could always trust her friends to be by her side when she needed them, and she knew that she needed them now more than ever.

TWENTY-THREE

Blu couldn't seem to get Gabby's sobs out of her mind, even though it had been several minutes now that she'd stopped crying in that way that worried Blu. The poor girl had been frantic as she'd run behind her father on the stretcher screaming that she wanted to go with him in the ambulance. It had taken both Isabella and Thomas to hold her back so that the ambulance could leave—and the promise from Blu that they'd arrive right behind them as she'd quickly grabbed her car keys.

She glanced at Gabby and Isabella in the review mirror, both with tear-stained faces, but Gabby's breathing under control now.

"Shh. He's going to be okay." Isabella whispered the words, and Blu imagined that she was speaking them for her own benefit as well as Gabby's.

Was he going to be okay? It had all happened so fast, each of them jumping into action, doing what they could in the split seconds after the ambulance had arrived.

"Gigi texted me that they are with Lia now. Antonio is

being seen and he did speak to Lia briefly after they arrived at emergency," said Isabella, looking at her phone.

"Bella, call Kylie, please, would you? She needs to know what's going on so she can get home right now." Blu was beyond irritated with her daughter for a variety of reasons, but after seeing how scared Gabby was, the most important reason at the moment was that Kylie understood that Gabby—that her family—needed her to be with them.

Isabella nodded as she held the phone up to her ear. "It's going straight to voice mail. I'll text her."

"Bella, do you really think my dad is going to be okay?" Gabby's voice was quiet.

"I do, yes. Gigi said that he spoke to your mom, so that's a good sign, right?"

Gabby nodded. "It was so terrible—when he fell like that in the sand. At first I thought he was only joking around—playing a joke on Arianna—but then he didn't get up."

"I know. I did too. It was scary—very scary. Honey, we just need to keep thinking all good thoughts, okay? And pretty soon you're going to be able to see him."

"I wish Kylie was here too. She always makes me feel better when I'm worried."

"I know." Isabella looked at her phone and shook her head. "We'll keep trying her."

Blu pulled into the parking lot of the emergency center, thankful that soon they'd be with Lia. She'd never seen Lia so pale as when she'd turned toward Blu in the kitchen—after they'd heard the sirens. She knew that Lia would need support and she was glad to be that for her. She'd promised Jemma that she'd keep them posted at the house. Jemma and Thomas had stayed back with the children.

Gabby and Isabella were out of the car and across the parking lot almost as soon as she pulled in. Blu grabbed her purse and made her way inside the emergency entrance, where she could see the girls already talking to Lia down the hallway. Blu hurried to hug her friend.

"Thanks for coming—for bringing the girls."

Lia still looked like she was in a bit of a daze.

"Of course," Blu said. "And you just let me know what you need. Are you hungry, Lia? Shall I go find some food somewhere?"

Lia shook her head. "No. No, I'm not hungry, and I want to be here when the doctor comes out—which should be any minute." She took Gabby's hand and they all followed her to the waiting room, where Gigi and Douglas were already sitting.

As Lia sat to talk with Isabella and Gabby, Blu made her way over to Gigi and Douglas. "Do you think it will be long? Before we know anything?"

"I don't know. He's been back there about twenty minutes, I'd say," said Douglas.

"He was talking when they brought him out of the ambulance. Well, at least he spoke a few words to Lia, which was great for her." Gigi looked over at their friend, who was up and pacing the small room. "I'm just going to go get her some water or something. I'm worried about her."

Blu nodded, settling back against the chair. "He is going to be okay, isn't he, Douglas?"

Douglas nodded, but Blu could tell by the look on his face that he felt the same concern—the same fears—as she did.

There was nothing to do but wait.

TWENTY-FOUR

Gigi had been by Lia's side when the doctor had come out to tell them the news. Antonio had had a massive heart attack. The fact that Thomas had been able to administer CPR had saved his life. Gigi had seen the instant tears in Isabella's eyes when the doctor had let them know. She had a lot to thank Thomas for—they all did.

They had enough information to know that Antonio needed bypass surgery and he needed it soon. Gigi had felt how stunned Lia was, the shock evident on her face and body as the doctor led her to where she could now see her husband.

"Do you think I'm going to be able to see him?" Gabby looked at Gigi with big eyes and she could feel her apprehension.

She reached over to hold her hand. "Yes, honey. I'm sure they'll let you see him before he goes into surgery. Let's just let your mom have a few moments alone with him."

She watched as Gabby pulled her phone out again—for about the tenth time since she'd sat down next to her. Gigi knew that she was trying to get a hold of Kylie, something that none of them had been able to do since leaving the house. Gigi also knew how angry Blu was with her daughter. For sure, things had gone too far now. The fact that Kylie had not responded to any of them was cause for concern, but with everything that had happened, there wasn't time just yet to be more worried than annoyed at her.

They all looked up as Lia entered the waiting room. She looked exhausted but there was a smile on her face. If Gigi had to bet, she'd say the smile was more for Bella and Gabby than anything Lia was probably feeling inside. If Antonio were about to have surgery, Lia would be worried.

"Gabby, honey—Bella—you can come now. Just for a few minutes, and then they are going to start prepping him for surgery." She looked over to where Gigi, Douglas, and Blu sat. "I'm sorry. The doctor made me promise that there wouldn't be more visitors—just for now. We'll all be able to see him soon though—after the surgery." She bit her bottom lip. "Gigi, can you please let the others now what's going on?"

"Don't you worry about anything. I've already let Jemma know and she'll relay it to everyone at the house. We're still trying to get a hold of Kylie, but Jemma is working on that too. You just go be with Antonio. Give him our love and tell him we are sending big hugs and prayers."

Lia nodded before she took Gabby's hand, leading her daughter and granddaughter out of the waiting room to where they could see Antonio.

"I'm going to go get a coffee. Can I get you both something?" Blu asked.

"No, I'm good for now, thanks," said Gigi.

"We'll go get something to eat once the girls are back, yes? I think we need to make sure that Lia is taking care of herself, and I'm sure that food is the last thing on her mind," said Douglas.

Gigi nodded and leaned over to give her husband a kiss on the cheek. "Thanks, honey."

He kissed her back and smiled. "For what?"

"Just for being here. You always make me feel so much better when things are unsettling."

Douglas grabbed her hand and held it tight. "There's nowhere else I'd be honey. And Lia is going to need us—all of us."

"It's a serious surgery, isn't it?" Gigi felt the tears forming in her eyes. She could so easily put herself in Lia's place; she knew how she'd feel if it were Douglas being prepped for open-heart surgery.

"It is, but Antonio is healthy. He'll get through it. People do, and I'm sure his odds are very good."

"Yes, we just have to stay positive, especially when Lia comes back out." Gigi squeezed his hand tightly. "I think this is all a bit of wake-up call, isn't it?"

"Yeah. Yes, I'd say it is. You just never know, do you?"

Gigi nodded and was quiet with her own thoughts while they waited for the others to come back out to the waiting room again. They were going to be in for a long day—and probably many days to come as Antonio recovered after his surgery.

Douglas had made some quick phone calls after they'd arrived—phoning his own doctor in San Francisco to be sure that the care Antonio was getting at this hospital was the best in the area. Gigi knew that Antonio was in good hands, and it was also good that he'd have them all nearby. If he had to spend a few months recovering from a major surgery, there were worse places he could be than where they were staying at the beach.

TWENTY-FIVE

Kylie grinned at Whitney as they made their way up the driveway in the taxi. They'd been out all morning and she'd finally insisted that they go back to her house because she'd forgotten to bring her phone charger with her. She felt a twinge of guilt when the house came into view.

She didn't like the way she'd left things with Gabby earlier, but that girl could be such a stick-in-the-mud at times. It was partly the reason she'd invited Whitney back to the house—in the hopes that if they spent a little time together, maybe the two of them could be friends.

"So, about Lance?"

"What about him?"

"Are you two officially a couple now or what?"

"What? No. I barely know him. I mean, maybe we're chatting a little bit, but nothing major. Besides, I'll be going home at the end of summer and I'm not sure that the long distance thing would be a good idea at all."

"Well, duh. Airplanes do go to Italy, you know." Whitney laughed, and Kylie was reminded that she wanted to ask her where she'd gotten her teeth whitened while she was in town. They were so perfect.

"Well, duh, I know that." Kylie grinned.

"But also, you don't want to tie yourself down either. You must be used to those very handsome Italian men. I could go for that—guys that are more mature and—you know, more cultured, I suppose. Guys like Lance are a dime a dozen around here. They just want to get tan, surf some waves, and show up at the cool parties in town."

"Well, I'd say that you do have a point."

The taxi stopped, Kylie paid the driver, and they both got out.

"Okay, so let me just check in with everyone and then we can go down to the beach or something. That's probably where Gabby and the kids are but I'll just check—plug my phone in."

Whitney wrinkled her nose.

"What?" Kylie laughed lightly but she wasn't sure that she was going to like what her friend had to say. "What's with the face? You don't want to go to the beach now?"

"No, I do. I'd just rather go back to where the others are. Not—well, you know, have it be all family time and stuff. If I'm being honest, Gabby seems like a huge bore and totally immature."

Kylie felt her heart beat a little faster and her voice came out quiet when she spoke. "No, she's not—well, maybe compared to a lot of your friends she is, but—but she's really nice. And the kids are great. Whitney, I can't not be around here at all."

"I know, I know—so you've said. Well, let's just put in a little time and then we can be back for the beach party that starts at four."

Kylie nodded. "Okay, that should be fine. Come on!"

They walked into the kitchen and the house was abnormally quiet.

"Hello? Anyone home?" Kylie called out. "Everyone must be at the beach, I guess." She opened the refrigerator and grabbed a can of soda. "Do you want one?"

Whitney nodded her head and followed her as she made her way to the stairs.

"Let me just grab a few things, plug in my phone..."

"Kylie?"

She could hear her sister calling down from the third floor.

"Yeah—I'll be up in a second," she called over her shoulder as they walked into her bedroom.

"Kylie, where have you been? We've all been trying to reach you and—" Jemma stopped talking when she noticed Whitney sitting on the bed. "Oh, sorry. Kylie, I need to speak with you. It's important."

Kylie looked from Jemma to Whitney, who had now stood up to walk over to the open door. "Hi, I'm Whitney." She stuck out her hand and Jemma barely took it for a second.

"Sorry, Whitney, I just really need to talk to Kylie for a minute."

"No problem." Whitney looked at Kylie. "I'll just go wait in the kitchen."

She left the room and Kylie shut the door after her, turning to glare at Jemma. "Wow, Jem, that was rude. What'd she ever do to you?"

"Kylie! How come you're not answering your phone? Even your texts? Do you not care about anyone except yourself?"

Jemma burst into tears and it shocked Kylie so much that her annoyance immediately turned to concern, as she sat down on the bed beside her sister.

"Jemma, what is wrong with you? I'm sorry for not getting back to you, but my phone died." She crossed the room to plug her phone into the wall, turning it on before she went back to sit by her sister on the bed. The minute she sat down, her phone notifications started dinging. "Wow! I guess you all *have* been trying to get a hold of me."

As she spoke the words, the fear was there. She looked at her sister and knew that something was wrong—something was really wrong. "Jemma, what's going on? You're scaring me."

Images of her parents raced through her mind. *Please, God, let them be okay.* She grabbed Jemma's hand. "What is it?"

"It's Antonio. He had a heart attack—on the beach this morning—everyone but me and Thomas and the kids are at the emergency room right now. He had to go in an ambulance and it was really very scary, Ky."

Kylie's heart was beating fast as the tears started to come. "Is he—is he going to be okay? Jem, is Gabby okay? She must be so scared."

Jemma nodded. "We think so. At least, that's what we are hoping. Thomas saved his life, actually—because he did CPR until the ambulance got here. If not for that—well, I don't think he would be alive right now."

"Thank God!" Kylie ran across the room to grab her phone, pulling up her text app and only spending a quick second to read Gabby's frantic texts to her, before texting her that she was on her way. She turned back to Jemma. "And now? What's happening now?"

"Well, Gigi phoned me a little while ago to say that he needed surgery. They're going to be prepping him for that any minute. I really want to get there myself actually, but someone needs to stay with the kids and—"

Kylie stopped in her tracks, suddenly feeling like the biggest jerk of all time. She hadn't been there for her family. Maybe not on purpose, but that was no excuse. It was like her mind cleared of this stupid fog she'd been living under and she remembered who she was.

"I can stay, Jem—with the kids if you want to go."

Jemma shook her head. "No, Rafael will be back soon and you should go. Go be with Gabby. I know it will mean a lot to her. She needs you."

Kylie nodded and swiped her hand across her face to wipe the tears away. She'd been a horrible friend to Gabby since she'd arrived. It was time to make it up to her.

TWENTY-SIX

Jemma hugged her sister close. Kylie was back. In that instant that they hugged, everything else fell away and she was that sweet little girl that was always so concerned about everyone else.

Kylie pulled back a bit to look at her. "I'm really sorry, Jem. I've been a jerk lately."

Jemma smiled. "Well, you have been a bit of jerk. But I knew that it was only temporary."

Kylie smiled too and then grabbed for her phone when it dinged. "Gabby says they're moving over to the hospital area— to another waiting room while Antonio's in surgery. She says she'll let me know where to meet them." She sent a reply back to her. "Oh crud, I forgot that Whitney is downstairs. I better let her know what's going on—so she can take a taxi or something to the beach. She didn't really want to be here anyway, so I'm sure she won't be bothered."

Jemma reached out to stop her from getting up off the bed. "Wait. Ky, I'm sorry if I've been hard on you. It's only because I've missed you." She reached under the collar of her shirt to pull out the necklace that she always wore, the dainty beads well worn between her fingertips, the color faded, but the message forever engraved in her mind. *My sister, my best friend.* "Do you remember giving this to me—when this was my bedroom and I was the one acting ridiculous?" She'd made so many mistakes back then, but the one thing she knew that she could always count on was the love and acceptance of her sister.

Kylie grinned and reached under her own collar to hold out the identical beaded necklace.

Time had passed and they'd both changed so much, but they'd always be there for one another. It was like that with all of them. And they needed to be there now for Antonio and his family—for their family.

Kylie pulled her in for one more big hug. "You're still my best friend, Jem—always."

"Me too. Now go! Get to the hospital and hug everyone for me. I'm going to be there shortly—after Rafael gets here to stay with the kids."

Kylie grabbed her phone and her purse and took off down the stairs. Jemma wasn't trying to eavesdrop but she couldn't help but catch some of the conversation between Kylie and Whitney downstairs in the kitchen. The words were loud and a bit harsh. It was obvious that Kylie's new friend wasn't happy with the change of plans and it was equally as obvious that Kylie didn't care what this Whitney girl thought about it.

She heard the honk of a car in the driveway and the front door closing shortly after.

Kylie would be there for Gabby. That was good.

Jemma would be ready to go just as soon as Rafael got home. Of course, she'd notified Chase and Rafael just as soon as everything had happened, but they'd gotten stuck in traffic and it was only a few minutes ago that Rafael had called to say they were about twenty minutes away.

She knew that it was important that she get to the hospital as well. They all needed to be there for Lia and Isabella.

"Mommy!" Chloe shouted to her from upstairs.

"Yes, darling?" She got up off Jemma's bed to make her way to the stairs.

"Mommy, the movie is over and the boys want to watch another one. Can we, Mommy?" Chloe was at the top of the stairs looking down at her.

"I'm coming up right now. See if you can choose one that is good for all of you."

"Not too scary, right, Mom?" Daisy called out.

"No. Nothing scary."

She settled the kids in with another video, telling them it was for a special occasion as so much TV time was not the norm for their family. She was lost in thought when Arianna got up from the floor to stand beside her.

"Jemma, can I sit in your lap, please?"

"Of course you can, sweetie." Jemma moved her phone from her lap to the table. "Come here." She gently pushed the little girl's hair behind her ears the way that the twins liked her to do. "Are you okay, honey?"

Arianna's lip trembled and a few tears slid down her cheeks. "I want my mommy."

"Oh, it's okay." Jemma leaned forward to kiss her on the forehead. "Your mom is at the hospital with your grandpa and grandma. Let me see if she can video chat with you, okay?"

Arianna nodded her head and Jemma sent off a text to Isabella.

"Ari, I bet that was kinda scary for you—when your grandpa fell down in the sand earlier."

She nodded her head. "Is Grandpa talking now?"

"Yes, honey. I think so. I think your Grandpa is going to be just fine. The doctors are going to work really hard to make him all better. We just need to be very patient and send him lots of prayers and good thoughts for his heart to become extra strong."

"Okay, I can do that."

Rafael appeared at the top of the stairs just when Arianna hopped off Jemma's lap to settle back on the bean-bag chair with Chloe in front of the TV.

"Hi, babe. I'm so sorry it took us so long to get here." Rafael bent down to kiss her before sitting close to her on the sofa, taking her hand in his. "Is there any news?"

Jemma shook her head. "No. Well, Gigi texted me about fifteen minutes ago that they were prepping him for surgery now. I guess it can take anywhere from three to six hours— they'll know more once he's on the table. So I think I should head over there. If you don't mind?"

"No, not at all. I'm sure Chase and I can hold down the fort here. And let us know if anyone needs anything." He looked at her intently. "Jem, he's going to be okay, isn't he?"

Jemma had been holding it together for so much of the day in front of the kids. That one question set her tears flowing again and she tried to remain quiet while they continued to watch their movie.

"I hope so, Raf." She buried her head against his chest, allowing a few minutes to feel his arms tightly around her before she got up to leave. "I really hope so."

TWENTY-SEVEN

Gabby looked around the waiting room, happy for the fact that they were all together—that they could all be there when her father woke up after surgery. Well, most everyone was there. But Kylie had said she was coming and that single text from her best friend had made all the difference to Gabby.

It had been both scary and comforting to see her dad before they'd taken him away to surgery. He'd looked so different—so frail and quiet. Both her mom and dad had assured her that everything was going to go just fine with the surgery but Gabby could see the fear in their eyes—and how hard it was for her mother to let go of his hand as they'd wheeled him away.

So now they would just have to wait.

A nurse had escorted them all over to a private waiting room of the hospital—one that was slightly bigger than what the other had been. There was a television on in one corner of the room and a bookshelf stacked with puzzles, board games, and every magazine that you could think of. Did people really play board games while waiting for loved ones to come out of surgery?

Maybe when the patient's chest wasn't open on the table—maybe when the surgery wasn't as serious as her father's was.

Gabby looked at her mother across the room talking to Jemma and she felt sick to her stomach for even having the thought. She had to stay strong for her mother. She could fall apart in the restroom if she needed to.

And also her father was going to be all right. He just had to be.

"Gabby!"

She turned toward Kylie's voice just as she ran into the room. During that one motion, at the sound of her name being called, Gabby burst into tears. Kylie's arms around her, hugging her tightly, had never felt so comforting. If ever Gabby had needed her best friend by her side, it was now, and she silently scolded herself for even doubting that Kylie would be there for her.

Kylie took her hand and led them both over to the small sofa in a quiet corner of the room. "Oh, Gabby, I'm so sorry." She hugged her close and then put some distance between them, her hands on Gabby's arms as she looked into her eyes. "He's going to be okay. I just know it."

Gabby could only nod her head, the tears still streaming down her face.

"Gabby, I'm so sorry that I've been such a jerk the past few days. Can you ever forgive me? I feel terrible for messing up our plan this morning, for the other night, for—well, just for everything, really. I know I've been horrid and it has nothing to do with you."

Gabby squeezed her friend's hand. "It's okay. I forgive you. That's what best friends do, right?"

Kylie nodded and wiped away her own tears. "You must

have been so scared—when it happened. I wish I had been there with you."

"Me too." Gabby whispered the words. "But you're here now and that's what matters." She leaned back against the sofa and closed her eyes. All that mattered was that her dad was going to get through the surgery without any problems. If that happened, Gabby knew that he would be all right.

TWENTY-EIGHT

Isabella ran to Thomas and wrapped her arms around him the moment he appeared in the doorway of the waiting room. Chase and Rafael had insisted that they could keep the children occupied—that Thomas should be there waiting with Isabella. She'd not seen him since they'd all left the beach behind Antonio in a stretcher that morning.

They were quiet for several seconds before Isabella felt Lia's arm come around her from behind. She quietly stepped aside as her grandmother embraced Thomas, weeping as she tried to get her words out.

"Thank you Thomas. I can never thank you enough. You saved his life."

Isabella wiped her own tears away as she saw the genuine love between two of the most important people in her life.

"I'm just glad he's okay, Lia—that he will be okay. He has you both have—so many people here sending love and prayers. He'll be back on his feet in no time."

Lia stood back just a bit, reaching her hand out for Isabella.

"I just—I thank God every day for bringing you into my life. I've never been so thankful."

Isabella nodded and reached out to hug her. "We love you. Everything's going to be just fine. We're going to make sure that Grandpa has the best care and really takes all the time to heal here that he needs."

Lia was nodding her head. "I believe that." She hugged Thomas again. "I'll give you two a little time. Thanks for coming, Thomas. It means a lot."

"Of course."

They both watched her walk back over to sit down next to Gigi and Douglas, and Isabella knew that they needed to try to keep her occupied for the next few hours, not that it could possibly take away any of the many thoughts that must be filling her head.

She felt the comfort of Thomas's arm come around her as he whispered in her ear. "How are you doing, honey? Are you holding up okay?"

She nodded her head. "Much better now that you're here. It's all so surreal. I just can't believe that Antonio is having major heart surgery right now." She shuddered at the words. She couldn't believe it, and she wouldn't let herself speak her worst fears out loud. What if he didn't make it? What if they left to go back to Italy without her grandfather? She shook her head as if doing so would rid her mind of such thoughts. She had to continue to pray and think only positive things.

"He's going to be okay, Iz." Thomas kissed her on the cheek and then smoothed her hair back from her face.

Isabella nodded. "I believe you. How was Arianna when you left? Jemma told me that she was pretty sad earlier. I think it was very scary for the kids—seeing Antonio like that."

"She seems fine now. I took her down to the beach for a few minutes before I left—to talk to her about sending prayers for Grandpa."

"Oh, I don't want her to worry. You don't think she's going to be traumatized, do you?"

Thomas shook his head. "No, she'll be okay, Iz. I told her that he was going to be just fine." He hugged her close to him, kissing her on the forehead.

"Yes, he will be." She looked at her grandmother sitting quietly across the room. "He just has to be."

TWENTY-NINE

Lia looked down at her husband where he lay in the hospital bed. The fear was mostly gone now, thanks to the doctor's words to her moments earlier.

She'd been sitting next to him—watching him—for several minutes now. She just needed for him to open his eyes and speak to her. Then she'd know it was for real.

As if reading her mind, Antonio's eyelids fluttered as he seemed to be trying to focus on her face.

She held his hand in hers, bringing his knuckles to her lips.

"Hey, you. I think it's time for you to wake up and talk to me."

He gave her a weak smile. "Hi, beautiful."

Lia moved aside as a nurse entered the room to check his vitals, getting him to sit up a bit in bed and drink a little water, a motion that made him gasp.

"Oh wow."

"I know," said the nurse. "It's going to get better. I promise. And I do have some pain meds for you. They'll help you get the sleep you need tonight." She turned toward Lia. "Did you want to spend the night in the room with him?"

"Oh, I didn't know that was possible." She nodded. "I'd like that very much, please."

"Okay, I'll have someone bring one of our cots in here. Assuming you have a good night, young man, we'll be moving you into a different room in the morning—for the duration."

"Which will be how long?" Lia asked. She couldn't wait to have Antonio out of the hospital because she knew how much it would start to bother him.

"Oh, I don't want to say for sure. The doctor will be able to give you a better idea, but most of our patients—the ones who do a good job of listening to their nurses anyway"—she winked at Antonio—"are generally discharged anywhere from three days to a week."

Antonio smiled. "Three days it is then. Captain."

He raised his fingers to his forehead in a solute and Lia laughed. "Well, we'll see about that. We don't need to be in any hurry. The most important thing is that you are getting the care you need, honey."

"No one can take as good of care of me as you, my love." He looked at the nurse, who had started toward the door. "No offense."

She laughed. "None taken." She winked at Lia. "I'd say you have a keeper there."

Lia smiled. "I sure do. He's not going anywhere."

Antonio smiled.

"So, I know a couple of girls who sure would love to see you awake—well, you have a whole waiting room out there, but we won't overwhelm you just yet. Can I bring Gabby and Bella in to see you, honey?"

"Yes, please. Poor Gabby. I know how much I scared her—must have scared all the kids. When I'm healed, I have to make it up to them with my sand castle building skills."

"Yes, well, you're going to be taking it easy for the rest of the summer if I have anything to say about it."

Antonio grinned. "Okay, darling. I'm listening."

Lia bent to kiss him gently on the lips before she left the room to get the girls, all the while thinking how lucky she was and how great Antonio always was about wanting to put her mind at ease. She knew that he was in pain. The doctor had told her that the healing process wouldn't be easy, especially for the first few days following surgery, but knowing Antonio, she'd only play a guessing game in terms of how much pain he was in.

This time, Antonio's stubbornness was not going to win out over Lia's determination that he listen and obey the doctor's instructions. She'd have him in full recovery mode for exactly the amount of time that the doctor prescribed and not one day less, no matter what Antonio had to say about it. And she was counting on the whole family to help her with the endeavor.

She was thankful they were all there at the beach house together. If Antonio had to be laid up for a period of time, it was the perfect place for his recovery. Lia had accepted Blu's offer to move them into the lower level suite, complete with a hospital bed that would be delivered that week. And it would be good for her too—to be surrounded by her friends. That alone, always made the hardest of times more bearable.

Lia entered the waiting room and all eyes turned toward her.

She smiled. "He's awake. He's talking. And he's going to be

okay." She wiped the sudden tears away as Gigi crossed the room to hug her close.

Yes, everything was going to be okay now.

THIRTY

Isabella watched her grandfather in the distance, grinning as the girls poured bucket after bucket of sand over his body. It was hard to imagine the state he'd been in two months earlier—after he'd had the heart attack. He'd been a surprisingly great patient, allowing them all to wait on him as he spent hours on the deck enjoying the sunshine and cool breeze.

Isabella smiled as Jemma came behind where she was standing against the railing of the deck to give her a quick squeeze.

"He looks great!"

"Doesn't he? To think how far he's come—since coming home from the hospital."

"I'm a bit shocked myself," Lia said as she stepped out onto the deck with a tray of food. "He's been a much better patient than I ever would have predicted."

Gigi and Blu appeared carrying a pitcher of lemonade and another tray of sandwiches and cookies.

"Well, I think he knew better than to mess with you." Gigi

laughed. "And I am not poking fun. I would have been exactly the same with Douglas as a patient."

"Me too," said Blu. "Girls, wanna come join us?"

"It looks so lovely," said Jemma.

"And fancy." Isabella smiled as she sat down next to Lia.

"Oh, I don't know about fancy, but it was nice of the guys to think of us, wasn't it?"

All the men had agreed that the women should have an afternoon together while they kept the kids occupied, so with Kylie and Gabby's help, they were having a picnic at the beach followed by an afternoon at the zoo.

"Yes, it was nice of them to think of us—and Gabby and Kylie too. I did tell the girls they could join us, but I think they quite liked the idea of spending the afternoon with the kids," said Lia.

"I'm just happy to see Kylie back to her normal self." Blu reached for a sandwich and laughed when she saw the funny look on Jemma's face. "What?"

"Oh, nothing. I'm happy too and yes, you were right—about her coming around. Well, let's just choose to believe that she would have done so with or without a crisis."

"Yes, of course she would have," said Gigi.

Jemma turned toward Isabella. "I'm so not ready for you to leave. Are you sure you guys can't stay another week?"

Isabella and Thomas were leaving in the morning with Lia and Antonio. Lia had insisted that Isabella should stay longer, but she and Thomas had discussed it and decided that it was best if they all returned to Italy together. Antonio had recovered quite nicely and his local doctor had given him the okay to travel, but it still didn't feel right just yet—sending them off without any support once they were home.

"No, we really do need to get back. But you guys are coming in a week, right? Let's make a plan to get the kids together not long after you're home. I know Arianna has been quite dramatic about how she feels having to leave the twins."

Jemma laughed. "I can relate. Chloe and Daisy have already been asking me when we are going to the vineyard."

Lia passed the plate of sandwiches across the table to Jemma. "Well, we'll just have to make that happen, then. You are all welcome whenever you're ready."

Isabella looked around the table at the women who'd come to mean everything to her. They were her family and she couldn't imagine a time that they'd not be there for one another. Since the day that she'd first met them, she'd felt an undeniable connection.

It was during times like this that Isabella thought about Arianna—about her birth mother—the most. Was this what Arianna had pictured when she'd written the letter to Isabella all those years ago? Isabella had reread the words so many times over the years that they were ingrained in her memory.

My greatest wish now is that you would know them all and be loved by them all the way that I was—and that they will have the chance to know you too.

It was hard to imagine that Arianna could have wanted anything else for Isabella. It was the greatest gift that she'd ever been given, and though it could never replace what it would have been to know her birth mother, this family that Isabella was a part of had eased that burden and changed her life.

"Bella, what is it?" Jemma squeezed her hand under the table. "Are you okay?"

Isabella nodded and wiped her hand across her cheek—wet

with tears that she hadn't even noticed. "Yes." She smiled and raised her glass of lemonade in the air.

"To the greatest women I've ever known. Thank you for loving me so completely."

She saw the quick glances among Lia, Gigi, and Blu as they lifted their glasses, with Gigi adding to the toast one of her own. "To Arianna, for bringing us all together."

Lia blew a kiss toward the sky. "You are forever in our hearts."

They clinked their glasses and Isabella knew that the moment—this moment on the deck of the beach house that Arianna had also loved—would become another memory in a long sea of memories to commemorate the wonderful times spent with her family.

"To Arianna."

THE STORY CONTINUES

In This Moment
Legacy Series, Book 14

Available on Amazon

PaulaKayBooks.com

IN THIS MOMENT — PREVIEW

Chapter 1

Gigi stood in front of her open suitcase, stepping back from the bed as she assessed the neatly folded clothes she'd laid out. She'd done this a hundred times—packing for Italy, for family gatherings, for the life she and Douglas had built between two homes.

Sausalito and Tuscany. California sunshine and Italian countryside.

The villa on Lia and Antonio's property had become a second home over the years—a place to return to whenever they needed family close. It should have felt routine by now.

So why couldn't she remember if she'd already packed her black sweater?

She looked down at the open suitcase, scanning the layers. Was it there? She carefully unfolded the top items—shirts, pants, her favorite scarf. And there, at the bottom, the soft cashmere sweater, already packed.

When had she done that? This morning? Last night? She remembered choosing it—remembered deciding she'd need it—

but the moment itself had slipped away, leaving nothing behind.

"Everything okay, love?"

Douglas appeared in the doorway, reading glasses perched on his nose, a sheaf of papers in his hand. Probably something about the vineyard accounts, or the Guatemala foundation. He'd never fully retired—not really. Staying busy gave him something solid to hold onto: meetings, numbers, plans. Ways to keep worry from settling too long.

Gigi smiled at him, smoothing the pile of clothes in the suitcase. "I'm fine. Just trying to decide what to bring. You know how I get."

He crossed the room and kissed the top of her head, lingering close enough that she felt his presence behind her.

"You could bring nothing," he said softly, "and Lia would still make sure you had everything you needed. She's like that."

"True." Gigi laughed, feeling the small knot in her chest loosen. "But I like to have my own things. You know me."

"I do know you." His voice was gentle, and when she looked up, she caught something in his expression. Concern? Tenderness? Both, probably. Douglas had always been able to read her better than she could read herself.

"What?" she asked.

"Nothing. I'm just excited to see everyone. It's been too long."

Eighteen months. It had been eighteen months since they'd all been together—the summer in San Diego when Antonio had his heart attack and scared them all half to death. They'd gathered around him then—the whole family—just like they always did when someone needed them. And he'd recovered beautifully, thank God. Strong as ever now.

But eighteen months was too long. Life got busy. Jemma had four kids to manage. Isabella was deep in the trenches of motherhood with her two little ones. Blu's fashion business kept her traveling. And Gigi and Douglas had their own rhythm now, splitting time between Sausalito and Tuscany, working with the orphanage in Guatemala when they could.

Still. Eighteen months.

"I can't wait to see the kids," Gigi said, zipping up one side of the suitcase. "Young Arianna must be so big now. And Samuel—two years old already. Can you believe it?"

"Time flies," Douglas said quietly.

"It really does." Gigi turned back to her dresser, opening the top drawer to grab her jewelry case. Where had she put it? She always kept it right here in the front left corner, next to her scarves.

She moved things around, frowning. Not there.

"Looking for something?"

"My jewelry case. The small brown one." She opened the second drawer, then the third. "I could have sworn I put it right here yesterday when I was organizing."

"Check the bathroom," Douglas suggested. "Didn't you wear your pearls the other day? Maybe you left it in there."

"Maybe." But she didn't remember wearing her pearls. When had she last worn them? Dinner with the Martins? No, that was weeks ago.

She walked into their bathroom, scanning the counter. There it was, sitting right next to her perfume bottles. The brown leather jewelry case, exactly where she must have left it.

Relief washed through her—followed immediately by something colder.

She picked it up and carried it back to the bedroom, tucking it into her carry-on bag. Douglas had returned to his papers, sitting in the reading chair by the window, but she felt his eyes on her.

"Found it," she said brightly.

"Good."

She continued packing—toiletries, medications, her favorite cardigan for the plane. The small things that made travel comfortable at seventy-two. Comfortable shoes. Reading glasses. Though where were her reading glasses? She touched her face, her hair—

Oh. They were on top of her head.

She pulled them down with a small laugh, catching Douglas's eye. He smiled at her, warm and easy, and she smiled back. No big deal. Everyone did that. It was normal.

"I made us some coffee," Douglas said, standing and stretching. "Want to take a break? We don't have to finish packing right this second."

"Coffee sounds perfect."

They walked downstairs together, Douglas's hand finding hers on the banister. The house smelled like the cinnamon candles she'd lit earlier, mixed with the cool bay air that always seemed to seep in through the windows. She loved this house. Her and Douglas's sanctuary. The place that held so many memories of her dear Arianna—the place Arianna had left her all those years ago.

Not because Arianna's belongings still lived here. Those had been packed away long ago, passed down, given new purpose. But the house remembered.

The kitchen where Arianna had once danced barefoot, music echoing late into the night.

The windows where she'd stood watching the fog roll in, arms folded tight against herself.

The quiet corners that had held laughter and grief in equal measure.

Leaving it—even temporarily—felt heavier than it used to.

In the kitchen, Douglas poured two mugs and handed her one, steam rising between them.

"To Italy," he said, lifting his mug.

"To family," Gigi said, clinking hers against his. "And to the new year. It feels right, doesn't it? Being together for New Year's —for New beginnings."

Douglas's expression flickered—they both knew the irony —but he smiled. "Yes, to new beginnings."

They sat at the small breakfast table overlooking the bay, the morning light dancing on the water. Sailboats drifted past, slow and peaceful. It was beautiful. It was home.

"Are you nervous?" Douglas asked after a moment.

"About the flight? No. You know flying doesn't bother me."

"Not about the flight." He set his mug down, his expression serious now. "About seeing everyone."

"Why would I be nervous about that?"

He didn't answer right away, just looked at her with those steady eyes that had seen her through so much. Her rock. Her partner. Her love.

"I just want to make sure you're okay," he said finally. "We can always postpone if you're not ready."

"Not ready for what? Douglas, what are you talking about?"

But even as she said it, she knew.

She could see it on his face. The concern he'd been trying to hide. The gentleness that felt almost like pity.

"I know it wasn't easy news to—"

"I'm fine," she said quickly. Too quickly. "The doctors said it's manageable. I'm on medication. I'm doing everything I'm supposed to do."

"I know you are." He reached across the table, covering her hand with his. "But that doesn't mean this is easy. And I don't want you to feel like you have to pretend with me."

Gigi looked down at their hands, his large and weathered, hers smaller, the skin paper-thin now and spotted with age. When had they gotten so old? It seemed like just yesterday they were newlyweds, dancing in this very kitchen, laughing about the future.

"I'm okay," she said softly. "Really, I am. It's just... little things. Nothing major... yet."

The word hung between them.

"But that's why I want to go now. While I can still enjoy it." She squeezed his hand. "While I'm still me."

His eyes filled, just for a moment, before he blinked it away. "You'll always be you. No matter what."

"I know. But..." She trailed off, unsure how to put it into words. The fear that lurked underneath everything now. The awareness that time was suddenly, acutely, finite. "I just want to see everyone. I want to be with our family. Can we just... can we just do that? Without worrying about the rest?"

Douglas lifted her hand to his lips and kissed her knuckles. "Of course. Whatever you want."

"I want to go to Italy. I want to eat Lia's cooking and drink Antonio's wine. I want to watch the kids play and listen to Blu and Jemma bicker like they always do. I want to hold little Arianna and hear her laugh." Gigi's voice caught. "I want to make memories."

"Then that's what we'll do," Douglas said firmly. "We'll make beautiful memories. All of us together."

They finished their coffee in comfortable silence, the kind that came from nearly twenty years of marriage, of knowing each other's hearts without needing to fill every moment with words.

When they went back upstairs to finish packing, Gigi felt lighter somehow. Determined. Yes, things were changing. Yes, the diagnosis had scared her—terrified her, if she was honest. But she wasn't gone yet. She was still here. Still Gigi.

She had time. Maybe years. Maybe less. The doctors couldn't say for sure.

But whatever time she had, she was going to live it.

She rummaged through her drawers, now looking for her scarf.

Douglas noticed but didn't say anything as he handed her the scarf she'd been looking for and kissed her temple.

"Ready?" he asked.

"Ready," she said.

Tomorrow they'd fly to Italy. Tomorrow they'd see their family again—all of them together under one roof. Tomorrow the real celebration would begin.

But tonight, she'd finish packing. She'd double-check everything, maybe even make herself a list. She'd go to bed grateful—for this house, for this man, for the life she'd lived.

And for the time she still had.

Chapter 2

Lia wiped down the worn wooden table near the window—

the one that had become the family table over the years. How many meals had they shared here? How many celebrations, tears, confessions, and toasts? The wood was smooth under her cloth, polished by years of use, marked with the invisible history of their family.

Through the window, she could see the Tuscan countryside rolling away in shades of winter grey and green. December was the quiet season—no tourists clogging the roads, no heat shimmering off the vineyard rows. Just the gentle rhythm of pruning and planning, of soups simmering and fires crackling. It was her favorite time of year, really.

"*Amore*, you're going to wear a hole in that table."

Antonio appeared from the kitchen carrying a crate of wine bottles, his strong arms making the load look easy despite his sixty-plus years.

Lia's breath caught before she could stop it, her hand lifting instinctively, as if she might steady him from across the room.

He set the crate down near the bar without so much as a wince, and only then did she let herself exhale as he crossed to her, his presence settling warm and familiar at her back.

"I want everything to be perfect," Lia said, leaning back into him.

"It will be. It always is." He kissed her neck. "Besides, they're family. They don't care if the tables are spotless."

"I care." She turned in his arms to face him. "It feels like it's been so long since we've all been together."

His expression softened with understanding. "I know. Too long."

"Much too long." She touched his face, feeling the familiar lines, the silver stubble she'd grown fond of in recent years. "After what happened to you in San Diego—"

"I'm fine. The doctors say I'm fine—strong as an ox, in fact." He flexed his arm playfully, and she swatted him.

"Don't joke. You scared us all half to death."

"But I'm here." He kissed her forehead. "And tomorrow, everyone else will be here too. Under one roof again. Just like old times."

Lia smiled, though her eyes stung with sudden emotion. Just like old times—except it was never quite the same, was it? The family had grown, changed, shifted. Children had been born. Couples had formed. Time had passed, leaving its mark on all of them.

She thought of Arianna, as she often did when the family gathered. How strange that a daughter she'd only known for a few precious months could still feel so present in her life. But Arianna had given her this—all of it. Her family, the restaurant, the vineyard—which had led her to Antonio and then to their daughter, Gabriela.

"What are you thinking about?" Antonio asked, reading her face the way he always could.

"Arianna. How she brought us all together."

"She did." His voice was gentle. "And we've honored her by staying together. That's what she wanted."

"I know." Lia stepped back, returning to her preparations. "I just hope—" She stopped herself.

"Hope what?"

"Nothing. Never mind." She moved to the next table, but Antonio caught her hand.

"Lia," he said gently. "What is it?"

She sighed, setting down her cloth. "I hope we don't lose this. The closeness. Life gets so busy, and eighteen months turns into two years, then three—and suddenly we're strangers who share a history but not a present."

"That won't happen."

"How do you know?"

"Because we won't let it." He pulled her close again. "Because this family—this beautiful, complicated, messy family —is the best thing any of us have. We all know that."

Lia wanted to believe him. And mostly, she did. But she'd lived long enough to know that life had a way of pulling people apart. Jobs, children, distance, priorities. It took work to stay connected. Conscious, deliberate work.

"You're right," she said finally. "And that's why I want everything to be perfect tomorrow. So they remember how good it feels to be together."

"Then let's make it perfect." Antonio kissed her once more and headed back toward the wine. "But first, let me know which bottles you want me to bring up. The Chianti Classico? The Brunello?"

"Both. And the Vernaccia for the white wine drinkers." She returned to her tables, her mind already running through the menu for tomorrow night's New Year's Eve dinner.

The door to the kitchen swung open and Gabriela emerged, her dark hair pulled back in a messy bun, her apron already splattered with flour.

"*Mamma*, I think I got the pasta dough right this time," she called. "Come taste?"

"*Un momento, tesoro.*" Lia finished with the table and followed her daughter into the kitchen, her heart swelling with the familiar pride and love she felt whenever she looked at the girl—no, the young woman—they'd adopted seventeen years ago.

The kitchen was warm and fragrant, filled with the smells of slowly simmering ragù, fresh herbs, and rising dough, the air alive with comfort and purpose. Lia's domain. Her art. The place where she expressed love through food, through tradition, through the careful alchemy of ingredients and time.

Gabriela held out a small piece of pasta dough, perfectly smooth and elastic.

Lia pinched off a bit and rolled it between her fingers. "Perfect," she pronounced. "*Brava*, my darling. You've been practicing."

Gabriela beamed. "I want to help more tomorrow. With the big dinner. Can I?"

"Of course. I'll need all the help I can get." Lia surveyed the prep work already underway—vegetables chopped and waiting, stocks simmering on the back burners, pastries cooling on racks. "We're making the cotechino tonight, yes?"

"Already started. It's in the pot." Gabriela pointed to the large stockpot on the stove. "And I bought extra lentils—just in case."

"Good girl." Lia rested her hand on her daughter's shoulder, grounding herself there for a moment.

Antonio poked his head through the door. "Lia, do you want the prosecco in the walk-in or should I leave some out to chill in the wine fridge?"

"Walk-in for now. We'll pull it out tomorrow afternoon." She wiped her hands on her apron. "And Antonio? Can you check that the heat is working properly upstairs? I want to make sure the private dining room is warm enough for the children."

"Already done. I turned it on this morning."

"What would I do without you?"

"Probably run this place twice as efficiently," he teased, disappearing back into the dining room.

Gabriela laughed. "He's not wrong. You're a little bit of a control freak, *Mamma*."

"I prefer detail-oriented." Lia returned to her mental checklist. "Now, let's talk about tomorrow's timeline. Everyone from Florence will arrive in the afternoon—Blu and Chase, Jemma and her crew. Isabella and Thomas are just down the road at the vineyard. Gigi and Douglas land in Florence in the morning, so they should be here by early afternoon as well."

"What about Kylie? She's coming, right?" Gabriela asked. The two girls had been best friends since childhood.

"She'll be with Blu and Chase. So you'll have your partner in crime back."

"We're not that bad," Gabriela protested, but she was grinning.

"You're terrible together. But in the best way." Lia smiled, remembering all the mischief the two had gotten into over the years. Nothing serious, just the normal chaos of childhood. Birthday parties and sleepovers, secrets and giggles—the bond between two girls who'd grown up close as sisters.

She turned her attention back to the stove, stirring the ragù and adjusting the heat. The sauce had been simmering since morning, the meat falling apart, the tomatoes reduced to a rich, dark red. Tomorrow she'd finish it with cream and fresh basil, serve it over the pasta Gabriela had made.

"*Mamma*?"

"*Sì?*"

"Do you ever worry?" Gabriela's voice was quieter now, uncertain. "That things will change? That we won't always have this?"

Lia looked at her daughter, seeing her own fears reflected there. "All the time," she admitted. "But you know what I've learned?"

"What?"

"Change is inevitable. People grow, circumstances shift. We can't stop time." She set down her spoon and took Gabriela's hand. "But we can choose how we show up for each other. We can make the effort. We can say yes when someone invites us to gather, even when it's inconvenient. We can put down our phones and be present. We can cook meals and share wine and tell stories until late into the night."

"That's what tomorrow is about?"

"That's what every gathering is about. Choosing each other, again and again." Lia pulled her daughter into a hug. "And this family? We're very good at choosing each other."

Gabriela hugged her back tightly, and Lia felt the truth of her own words settle in her bones. Yes, it had been a long time. Yes, she worried about distance and all the things that could pull them apart.

But tomorrow they'd all be here. In this restaurant, around these tables, sharing this food. And for however many days or hours they had together, they'd remember why they did this. Why they kept coming back to each other, year after year.

Because Arianna had taught them that family wasn't just about blood. It was about love. About showing up. About making the choice, over and over, to belong to each other.

And they would keep choosing. Lia would make sure of it.

"*Andiamo*," she said, releasing Gabriela and returning to the stove. "We have work to do. This dinner won't cook itself."

They worked together in comfortable rhythm, mother and daughter, preparing for the feast to come. Outside, the winter light began to fade, painting the hills in shades of lavender and gold. The restaurant grew warmer as the ovens worked, as the pots bubbled, as the promise of tomorrow filled every corner.

By the time Antonio came back to announce he'd finished setting up the dining room, Lia felt ready. More than ready.

Let them come. Let them fill this space with laughter and noise and love. Let them eat and drink and remember why they belonged to each other.

Life changed in a moment—she knew that better than anyone. But some things remained constant.

Family. Food. Love.

And the choice to show up, no matter what.

A NOTE FROM THE AUTHOR

Thank you so much for reading *A Summer Together.*

If you've fallen in love with these characters and the world of the Legacy Series, I'd love to invite you deeper into the story.

I've written a quiet, emotional prequel titled *Out of Time* that sheds light on the relationships, choices, and moments that shaped everything that follows.

As a thank-you for joining my reader list, you can receive *Out of Time* as a free digital gift, along with future updates and special releases from the Legacy Series and my other women's fiction.

To receive your free prequel, please visit:
PaulaKayBooks.com

I'm so glad you're here.

—Paula

ABOUT THE AUTHOR

Paula Kay writes women's fiction about family, friendship, and the quiet moments that shape who we become.

Her Legacy Series explores love, loss, and the ties that bind us across generations, with settings inspired by Italy, San Francisco, and the places that feel like home long after we've left them behind.

When she's not writing, Paula enjoys meaningful conversations, books that make her cry, and a little too much reality television.

PaulaKayBooks.com

ALSO BY PAULA KAY

Legacy Series:

Book 1: *Buying Time*

Book 2: *In Her Own Time*

Book 3: *Matter of Time*

Book 4: *Taking Time*

Book 5: *Just in Time*

Book 6: *All in Good Time*

Book 7: *Bella's Hope*

Book 8: *Bella's Holiday*

Book 9: *Bella's Heart*

Book 10: *Bella's Home*

Book 11: *Christmas in Tuscany: A Legacy Series Reunion*

Book 12: *Birthday Surprise: A Legacy Series Reunion*

Book 13: *A Summer Together: A Legacy Series Reunion*

Book 14: *In This Moment: A Legacy Series Reunion*

Book 15: *Where It Began: A Legacy Series Reunion*

The Nomadic Sisterhood:

Know by Heart

Stay the Course

Clear the Air

Lost for Words

Out of Touch

Turn the Tide

Rock the Boat

Back on Track